CRY DANGER

"Perhaps it was that girl, the one who vanished," whispered Jenny.

"Or her ghost," said Joanne.

"Or her murderer!" said Ami softly.

Everyone turned and stared at Ami and then, with ear-splitting shrillness, Joanne and Jenny screamed.

Sophie fell silent.

She felt cold suddenly.

Deathly cold.

Hippo Mystery

CRY DANGER

Ann Evans

Scholastic Children's Books
7–9 Pratt Street, London NW1 0AE, UK
a division of Scholastic Publications Ltd
London ~ New York ~ Toronto ~ Sydney ~ Auckland

First published by Scholastic Publications Ltd, 1995

ISBN 0 590 13163 X

Typeset by TW Typesetting, Midsomer Norton, Avon
Printed by Cox & Wyman Ltd, Reading, Berks.

*For my husband John and our
children Wayne, Angela and Debbie*

CHAPTER 1

"We must be crazy! Absolutely crazy!"

"Stop worrying," said Sophie, glancing back between the head rests. "It happened over a year ago, that's if it happened at all."

Sophie's classmates, Jenny and Joanne, sitting behind in the minibus, exchanged glances.

"But it's true," argued Jenny. "I even heard the Head whispering to Miss Mooney about it, when we stopped at that service station a while back."

"Rubbish!" Sophie laughed and nudged Ami, her best friend. "Honestly, that pair! They'd believe anything."

"They're not *still* going on about that girl, are they?" Ami asked.

Sophie nodded. "Just because some girl vanished from this Plas Dol-y-Mynydd house we're holidaying at, they think we're all going to vanish into thin air like she did."

Ami lowered her voice creepily. "Maybe we will, at least, one of us."

"Oh, shut up, Ami," Sophie said, digging her friend in the ribs. "She probably just ran away."

Jenny poked her head around the seats. "But no one's seen her since."

"That doesn't mean anything sinister happened to her."

"She could have had an accident," Joanne suggested. "Perhaps she got lost in the mountains or something."

"It's possible," said Sophie.

"But why hasn't she ever been found?" asked Jenny.

"I don't know, Jen," said Sophie. "But you mustn't let it spoil your holiday."

Ami's eyes flashed. "But what if she didn't

run away? What if she didn't have an accident? That leaves only one thing…"

"Ami!" warned Sophie.

"She must have been m—!"

Sophie silenced her by clamping a hand over her best friend's mouth. "Shut up, Ami, will you! You'll have Jenny and Jo scared to death."

Ami began to chuckle and Sophie dug her playfully in the ribs again. They settled down then in cheerful silence as the bus veered off the main road and bumped its way along narrow, twisting lanes, travelling deeper into the rugged Welsh countryside.

As the sun slowly set, casting long shadows across the moors, Miss Mooney, their new English teacher, made her way down the aisle of the bus, swaying like a long slender twig in a breeze as the bus bounced along the track.

Miss Mary Mooney had been with Stansfield Comprehensive for almost eight months. Rumour had it that her fiancé left her for another woman some time last year, so she'd moved south to start a new life.

"It'll not be long now, girls," Miss Mooney informed them in her broad Geordie accent as she gave Sophie's long red hair a playful tug. "You'll have to tie this back, Sophie. You'll be getting it tangled up in branches and rocks and goodness knows what else."

"Yes, miss," Sophie answered, wondering why Miss Mooney didn't do something more adventurous with her own straight mousy hair than fastening it back in an elastic band.

"Miss," came a shout from the back of the bus. "Will we be going abseiling?"

"Hopefully," smiled Miss Mooney.

"And canoeing?" asked another.

"Yes."

"And climbing?"

"I believe so."

"And horse riding?"

"Probably. Now look, girls, we'll be arriving at Plas Dol-y-Mynydd House very soon, and I believe Mr Meredith will have a full activities schedule all worked out."

"Who's Mr Meredith?" asked Sophie eagerly.

A pink blush coloured Miss Mooney's pale cheeks. Her voice seemed to soften. "Mr Meredith is the instructor at the House. He organizes all the activities for the children who holiday there."

"Please, miss," Joanne called, as Miss Mooney was about to return to her seat.

"Yes, Joanne?"

"Miss, is it true that a girl vanished from Dol-y-Mynydd last year?"

A hush fell over the minibus. Twelve young faces sat goggle-eyed, waiting for Miss Mooney to reply.

The colour drained from her face. Her mouth dropped open although no sound came out of it. There was a flash of bright blue tracksuit as Mr Granger, the games teacher, jumped to her aid, but the Headmaster caught hold of his arm.

"I'll deal with this," the Head said, squeezing between the rows of seats. He tapped Miss Mooney on the shoulder. "Sit down, Mary, I'll speak to the girls."

Looking relieved, she returned to her seat.

The Head cleared his throat. "Now then, girls, I gather you've all heard the rumours, so let me put your mind at rest. I don't want you worrying unnecessarily. Nevertheless, it is a fact that a girl did mysteriously disappear from Plas Dol-y-Mynydd house."

A hubbub of chatter sprang up.

"Quietly now!"

Silence descended again. You could have heard a pin drop.

"A year ago," said the Headmaster, "a fifteen-year-old girl from St. Mark's Convent up on the north-east coast went missing on the last day of her holiday. Despite an intense search and extensive enquiries, she was never seen again."

More gasps.

"You may have read in the papers that Plas Dol-y-Mynydd house was closed for some months while police searched the area. It re-opened at the beginning of this year and hundreds of youngsters have enjoyed adventure holidays there all year." He peered over his spectacles at every one of them. "So there is no reason for you girls to be troubled by past events."

"See," murmured Sophie reassuringly. "Told you we'd nothing to worry about."

"However," continued the Head.

"Uh-oh," groaned Joanne.

"I don't want any of you wandering off. You work in groups. And always let myself, or a member of staff, or Mr Meredith our instructor, know where you are going. Is that understood?"

"Yes, sir," everyone answered together.

"Good! Ah, I believe we're almost here."

Joanne peered around the seats. "See! He's scared in case one of *us* goes missing."

Sophie groaned. "He's just talking common sense. Isn't he, Ami?"

Ami was bent, head between her knees, fiddling with her bag. She didn't reply. Sophie turned her attention to Plas Dol-y-Mynydd house as it came into view.

In the misty twilight, it looked far from welcoming. More like something out of a horror film. Surrounded by black shadowy trees, the sharp pointed turrets on the roof and long tall chimney pots created an eerie silhouette against the red streaked sky. Everyone fell strangely silent.

Suddenly Ami leapt to her feet and pointed agitatedly through the bus window. "Look, up there on the roof!"

"What?"

"What can she see?"

"I can't see anything…"

"There!" Ami cried again. "Behind the chimney. A man. Wearing a black cloak. Look … look … he's flying! No, it's not a man…" She spun round to face everyone and shrieked, "It's Count Dracula!"

The entire bus erupted in an ear-splitting scream of terror.

CHAPTER 2

When the screaming finally stopped, Ami remained arms outstretched, fake plastic fangs sticking out of her mouth and two lines of red lipstick streaked down her chin.

Groans and laughter replaced the screams and Ami was bombarded with rolled-up sweet papers.

Struggling to keep a straight face, the Headmaster said sternly, "Very amusing, Ami. Now kindly take those teeth out before you choke on them, and the rest of you please settle down and behave."

"You nutcase!" laughed Sophie.

"It got them going, didn't it?"

"You might have warned me," Sophie complained, gathering her belongings as the bus lurched to a halt.

They filed off the bus and stood in excited little groups as their luggage was unloaded. Then, weighed down with holdalls and suitcases, they trudged slowly towards the old house.

The smell of woodsmoke and pine trees filled the air. Dense woodlands surrounded the old house. Gnarled elms with twisted branches that looked like old men's arms. And oaks with strange faces etched into the bark.

"It's spooky," Ami hissed.

"It'll look different in the daytime," Sophie murmured hopefully.

"It'd better, or I'm catching the first train home," added Joanne.

A heavy hand came down suddenly on Sophie's shoulder. She turned quickly. "Oh, it's you, Mr Granger!"

The games teacher's bushy brown beard parted in a grin as he fell into step with the girls. "Scare you, did I? Sorry. Well, what do you think of your new home for the next two weeks?"

"Probably haunted," Ami said cheerfully.

"Yes, by the ghost of that girl," muttered Joanne.

"There's no proof that she's dead, Jo," said Sophie. "I bet she just ran away."

Mr Granger stroked his beard thoughtfully, and, talking more to himself than anybody, said, "A real mystery that. I can't understand where she went."

"Did you know her then, sir?" asked Sophie.

"No, not personally. Why do you ask?"

Sophie shrugged. "I don't know. It was just the way you spoke of her."

"No. I never knew the child." He turned his attention to the house. "Ah, it looks like a welcoming party."

A blaze of light flooded from an open doorway. It illuminated the wide flight of stone steps that led down from the main entrance. Stone pillars with ornate lions' heads stood either side of the step – looking majestic – standing guard.

Silhouetted against the light appeared a giant of a man. He stood for a moment, looking down at the newcomers. Then he strode down the stone staircase, seeming to grow more immense with every step.

He wore jeans and a lumberjack shirt, the sleeves rolled up past his huge biceps. He towered over everyone, even Mr Granger. And he had a face that looked as if it had been chiselled from stone just like the lions' heads. His eyes were as black as his hair. His gaze swept over them all. He paused as he caught sight of Miss Mooney.

"Mary. It's good to see you again," he said in a deep Welsh accent.

"David," Miss Mooney murmured, buckling slightly at the knees.

Ami nudged Sophie. "She fancies him."

His black gaze continued its sweep over everyone's upturned faces. It paused momentarily upon Mr Granger, as if the man was trying to recall where he'd seen him before.

Then, dismissing the notion, it swept on.

The instructor's foreboding eyes finally settled heavily upon Sophie. She swallowed nervously, unsure whether to smile or cringe. Behind her, whispering and giggling broke out and she fidgeted uneasily under his intense scrutiny. Her cheeks were flaming when he finally dragged his eyes off her and spoke to the whole group.

"My name is David Meredith," he announced, standing, legs astride, hands on hips, looking powerful and dangerous. "I am your instructor. While you are here, you will follow my rules and do precisely what I tell you. Is that understood?"

"Yes, Mr Meredith," answered twelve small voices.

"I hope you mean that," he said fiercely, "because I stand for no foolhardiness. No stupidity. No misbehaving. Am I making myself clear?"

"Yes, Mr Meredith," everyone answered again.

"Good. Follow me then. There's a meal

ready for you. After which you can settle into your dormitories. An early night is what you need after your long journey." Turning, he led the way back up the steps.

"Why did he stare at you like that?" Ami asked, as they filed into the house behind him.

"I don't know, do I?" Sophie answered, still flushed from the scrutiny of those intense, dark eyes.

The kitchen was warm, bright and welcoming. A log fire crackled in a huge old-fashioned grate, tables were set and there was a delicious aroma of roast potatoes.

When everyone was assembled, David Meredith introduced the cook, a plump, red-cheeked lady whose eyes sparkled as he put a muscled arm around her chubby shoulders.

"Girls! This is Mrs Golightly. She will be preparing your evening meals and packed lunches. Breakfasts, however, and all washing up, will be done by you on a rota basis. You'll find this rota pinned inside your bedroom doors along with an agenda of activities for the week."

"Well, I'm not arguing with *him*," whispered Ami.

"Me neither," echoed Joanne.

Dinner was good but it came as an anti-climax when Sophie and Ami discovered they were first on the washing-up rota – and last to settle into their dormitory.

They were sharing with Jenny and Joanne on the ground floor at the far end of the corridor. The other two had already unpacked and were busy complaining about the lumpy mattresses and coarse blankets when Sophie and Ami finally joined them.

Sophie studied the activities agenda. "This sounds great. Day one, gorge walking. Day two, rock climbing." Her face dropped. "They won't be taking us too high, will they? Ah well, let's see – day three, horse riding – great! Day four, canoeing, day five…"

"I wonder if this is the bed where the girl slept before she vanished," Ami interrupted in a low, creepy voice. "Perhaps she's still here. Look under your beds, everyone."

Joanne did just that and Sophie laughed.

"Ignore her, Jo, she's just being her usual stupid self."

"Mock if you like," hissed Ami, "but I think the body of that girl is still here … somewhere. Tucked away in a cupboard maybe, or nailed under the floorboards. Waiting to leap out at some unsuspecting person."

"It can hardly leap anywhere if it's dead," Sophie remarked. "Anyway, shut up about it or we'll all be having nightmares."

But Ami merely spoke in a more deathly whisper. "Well, I think we should search the room. Look under all the beds, in the wardrobes, behind the curtains…"

"Ami!"

"I know a scary story," Jenny said gleefully, leaping on to Ami's bed by the window.

"Let's hear it," said Ami, switching off the light. "Then I'll tell you a really spooky one."

Joanne looked doubtful, but with a pillow to hug, she joined the others on the bed.

"You start," said Ami to Jenny.

"OK then. It was a dark, dark night…"

Ami instantly interrupted. "Oh, not the one about the dark, dark house, and in the dark, dark house was a dark, dark cupboard, and in the dark, dark cupboard…"

"No!" Jenny said indignantly. "It's not that one. This is about my aunt and uncle."

"Sorry. Go on then."

"Right. Well one dark night they stopped in this really old house, and in the night, my aunt woke up and saw a shadowy figure of an old man standing over my uncle's bed."

"What happened?" Joanne whispered, chewing the corner of the pillow.

"She shouted for my uncle, and the shadowy figure turned and smiled and then just faded away."

"Honestly?" Joanne gasped.

"'Course not," Sophie argued. "There's no such thing as ghosts."

"Want a bet?" Ami said in her most spooky voice. "Then let me tell you about the phantom coachman. It was midnight, snow lay thick on the ground…"

Sophie had heard this story before. Not to

spoil the atmosphere, however, she sat with her knees hunched under her chin, trying to look interested. But her attention wandered to the chink in the curtains where a shaft of bright moonlight filtered in.

"...six silver horses pounded the country road..." Ami went on.

Hope it doesn't rain this week, Sophie thought to herself, looking forward to the activities that were planned. Canoeing would be fun.

"...yet they left no hoof prints in the snow..."

Not too sure about rock climbing, thought Sophie, who had always been a little afraid of heights. But going horse riding again would be fantastic.

"...and when the coachman looked back," continued Ami, holding the other two captivated, "they saw he had no face..."

The shaft of moonlight through the curtains was blocked suddenly, throwing them all into pitch blackness. A twig snapped outside the window.

Jenny and Joanne shrieked.

Sophie scrambled over the bed. Pulling the curtains wide she peered out into the darkness. "There!" she cried. "There's someone running towards the woods."

"Where?"

"I can't see…"

"Look, there!" Sophie shouted. "Can't you see, just ducking behind the trees."

"Who was it?" Ami demanded, clambering over Sophie's back to get a better look.

"I don't know. But he was outside our window."

"Who? Who could it have been?" Joanne whispered, her voice quivering with fear.

"I couldn't tell."

"Perhaps it was that girl, the one who vanished," whispered Jenny.

"Or her ghost," said Joanne.

"Or her murderer!" said Ami softly.

Everyone turned and stared at Ami and then, with ear-splitting shrillness, Joanne and Jenny screamed.

Sophie fell silent.

She felt cold suddenly.
Deathly cold.

CHAPTER 3

Everyone came running.

First the other girls, wanting to know what had happened. Then the Head, looking like a big round lollipop in his candy-striped pyjamas. Mr Granger switched on the light. His cheeks were red, as if he'd been running a long way rather than just along the corridor. Finally, David Meredith shouldered his way through the crowd that had gathered in the doorway. He looked directly at the four girls huddled by the window. Once again, Sophie felt his black gaze bore into her.

She shivered.

"What's going on? What's all this scream-ing?" the Head demanded, squinting until he had found his spectacles in his pyjama pocket.

"There was someone outside our window, sir," Sophie explained quietly.

David Meredith cast one last sweeping look around everyone in the room and strode out, apologizing to Miss Mooney as he bumped into her in the corridor.

"Wasn't *he* interested!" Ami grumbled sarcastically.

"Shut up," Sophie said. "He's probably going to search the grounds."

"I think he's going back to bed."

Miss Mooney was the only other member of staff dressed for bed, however. In dressing-gown and slippers, she efficiently dispersed the girls back to their rooms with words of reassurance.

Mr Granger moved the curtains aside. "What exactly did you see then, girls?"

"We heard a twig snapping outside the window, sir," Sophie explained. "It must have been a person, because he blotted out the moonlight for a second."

Mr Granger studied the angle of the light filtering in. "Not a child then, obviously someone tall."

"I saw someone running into the trees over there," Sophie added.

"A man?"

"I couldn't tell."

Mr Granger hurried towards the door. "I'll go and help Meredith search the area. "And, taking a torch from the pocket of his track-suit, he dashed out.

Miss Mooney shuffled back. "Come on now girls, get yourselves into bed and stop your worrying. I'm sure it was nothing."

"But Sophie saw someone running away," Ami wailed.

Mary Mooney smiled gently and tucked the sheets around each of the girls in turn. "I think you've all had a long tiring journey. I also think you've got over-active imaginations." She stroked Sophie's long red hair back from her anxious eyes. "Go to sleep. Tomorrow, you'll have forgotten all about this. Good night, girls."

"Good night, Miss Mooney."

She switched off the light.

Sophie waited until she could hear the steady breathing of the others before she climbed out of bed again. She turned on the light and stood, looking down at the wooden floorboards.

"What are you doing?" Ami murmured sleepily.

"Nothing," Sophie answered as she switched the light off again and climbed back into bed.

She lay awake, listening to the sounds of the night. The faint howl of wind that found a crack in the window to whistle through. The distant mournful bleating of sheep on the moors.

She tried not to let it bother her – the fact that she had seen the outline of wet footprints on her bedroom floor, left by someone who had been in her bedroom just a short while ago.

Wet footprints, and little bits of damp grass, left by someone's shoes.

Someone's shoes which had very recently been outside.

Outside their window maybe?

CHAPTER 4

"What's gorge walking?" Ami asked, as they all gathered outside Plas Dol-y-Mynydd house after breakfast the next morning.

Dressed in hiking boots, jeans, warm sweaters and armed with waterproofs and a packed lunch, Sophie decided that whatever it was, they could handle it.

She felt much happier this morning. The sun was shining and she had decided to dismiss last night's events as a figment of her imagination. Even the house looked friendlier in daylight.

Last night she hadn't spotted the sloping green lawns and flowers beds. Nor the ornamental pond, alive with newts and frogs and dragonflies. But more especially, she hadn't glimpsed the magnificent view of purple hills and majestic mountains whose peaks speared the fluffy white clouds. Even their instructor didn't seem quite so terrifying.

David Meredith jogged down the steps. At his side tripped Miss Mooney. They were chatting away like old friends.

"I think you could be right," Sophie whispered to Ami.

"What about?"

Sophie nodded towards the happy couple. "Our instructor and Miss Mooney. She must have been here before. Perhaps they're in love!"

Ami raised her eyebrows and looked away. In a tiny voice she said, "Well, maybe Miss Mooney's in love, but as for him, I reckon he's got a thing about young redheads."

"What?"

"He's staring at you again."

"Don't be stupid…"

Sophie's voice trailed away. He *was* staring.

Miss Mooney was still nattering on, only he wasn't paying the slightest bit of attention. He was too preoccupied with staring at Sophie.

As Sophie began to feel her cheeks turning as red as her hair, she spotted the Head in his new bright orange tracksuit strolling along with Mr Granger. She ran across the lawns to meet them.

"I like your tracksuit, sir," she said breathlessly, turning her back on David Meredith.

"Thank you, Sophie, it was a gift from my wife." He rubbed his hands together. "Are we all set?"

"Yes, sir," everyone answered.

She didn't hear David Meredith join them, and jumped when his deep Welsh tones rang in her ear. But to her relief, he hadn't come to speak to her, but to Mr Granger.

"I've been meaning to speak to you, Mr Granger. You see, I've this funny feeling that we've met before. Have we?"

As Paul Granger stroked his beard thoughtfully and shook his head, Sophie made her getaway. That man unnerved her!

The teachers didn't spend long chatting. Moments later, David Meredith was addressing the whole group.

"If we're all assembled, we'll get on our way then," he announced. "I'll lead and a member of staff will bring up the rear. You girls will remain somewhere between us. You will not wander away from the group. Is that clear?"

"Yes, Mr Meredith," everyone echoed.

He strode ahead, his long athletic legs covering the ground so swiftly that everyone had to practically run to keep up. They took a path through the woods, where silver birch and dark oaks wove a canopy of branches to shade them from the bright sunlight.

Eventually the woods gave way to fields and hills. For as far as the eye could see were gently rolling moors smothered in coarse grasses and ferns. Low slate walls divided them into a patchwork of greens and purples and browns. Wild flowers grew everywhere and woolly sheep grazed contentedly.

They stopped for lunch by a stream. Afterwards, David Meredith got to his feet.

"We're not far from the gorge now," he said, looking like Goliath as he towered over them. "The water's not deep but it's a very rocky winding area, so we'll progress in small groups. One adult to three girls. I'll take you, you and you."

He pointed to Sophie and two others.

"Me?" she murmured, aware of a sinking sensation in the pit of her stomach.

"Yes, you. Come along girls, sort yourselves out."

Ami dug her in the ribs. "Now how did I guess he was going to pick you?"

"Oh, why me?"

Ami grinned. "Be good!"

Reluctantly, Sophie joined her two classmates and David Meredith. The other two seemed delighted to have been chosen.

Sophie found herself studying his feet and wishing she'd measured the size of the footprints in her room last night.

"All ready?" David Meredith asked.

Sophie looked up quickly, embarrassed at being found studying his feet. "Yes, all ready."

Her uneasiness faded when they reached the gorge. It was fantastic. A deep ravine that led down to a crystal clear stream. And craggy walls of grey rock, smothered in mosses and ferns and wild flowers. Waterfalls rushed down from the rocks. Some just trickles, others quite awesome, one so large they were able to walk behind it.

In the dark echoing cavity behind the thundering wall of water, Sophie was glad that David Meredith was their guide. His steadying hand, helping them over the slippery rocks, was reassuring. And when they emerged into the sunshine, she actually found herself smiling up at him.

"We'll rest here a while and wait for the others to catch up," he said, stretching out on the grass.

Sophie sat a little way off, threading a blade of grass with her thumbnail. Her two classmates threw pebbles into the stream.

"It's Sophie, isn't it?" David Meredith said in his deep Welsh accent.

"Yes."

"Is it your first time here, Sophie?"

"Yes," she answered again, feeling so over-awed by his presence that she couldn't think of one intelligent thing to say.

"And what are your impressions so far?"

"Very good," she answered, searching for something interesting to say. "I ... I'm looking forward to going horse riding."

"Can you ride?"

Her eyes lit up. "Yes, I've been riding since I was quite small. I love it. I was wondering about rock climbing though." Sophie looked towards the distant rocky peaks. "We won't be tackling any of those, will we?"

For once, David Meredith laughed. "Don't worry, that kind of mountain is for the experienced climber, not the likes of you, Sophie."

She breathed a sigh of relief. "Thank goodness for that."

Mr Granger's group appeared then from behind the waterfall. Sophie scrambled to her feet. "Ah, here they come!"

David Meredith stood behind her, like a mountain himself, staring over her head. "How long has Mr Granger been teaching at your school?"

Sophie shrugged. "I'm not sure, a couple of months about. Why?"

The instructor's black eyes were narrowed against the glare of the sunlight reflecting off the waterfall. Softly, he said, "I was just wondering, that's all. Just wondering."

When everyone had gathered, they set off once more. Enjoying the labyrinth of streams and valleys, exploring caves and rocks. The sun was low in the sky when they finally turned for home.

"I'm exhausted!" declared Ami as they dragged their weary feet homeward.

They were walking now in a straggling line. David Meredith was in the lead, way ahead. The staff and the rest of the girls were ambling along behind him. Sophie and Ami trailed along at the back, with nothing behind them but the Welsh hills.

Crumbling slate walls lined their route. Beyond these were fields of sheep, and rough earth smothered in heather and thistles.

A movement just behind a low wall caught Sophie's eye. At first she thought it was a sheep. Then she spotted the hunched shoulders of someone scurrying alongside. Her heart gave a painful thud. She grabbed Ami's arm and hissed, "Ami! There's someone behind that wall. Someone's trailing us."

"You're joking!"

"No joke. Quick, let's catch up with the others."

But before they had run more than three steps, the figure vaulted the wall and stood before them.

Barring their escape.

CHAPTER 5

"What do you want?" Sophie asked, her heart thudding so loudly she could actually hear it.

He was about seventeen, tall and slim with bright copper-coloured hair and eyes so pale they could almost have been silver.

"What do you want?" Sophie repeated, her voice rising.

He said nothing but stood there, staring at her with those strange silvery eyes.

"Helena? Is that you?" he said, at last.

Sophie frowned. "No. There's no one here called Helena. Would you let us pass, please?"

A look of disappointment darkened his face.

"I thought … hoped." He looked agitated, his silver eyes darting back to the rest of the group.

"What?" Sophie asked. "What did you hope?"

"Look, just get out of the way, would you," Ami snapped. "Or we're going to shout for help."

"Who *are* you?" Sophie asked gently, no longer afraid of this boy, but wildly curious.

"Doesn't matter who I am," he said in an accent similar to their instructor's.

"Why were you following us?" Ami demanded. "What do you want?"

His silver eyes flashed again. "Be careful, be very careful while you're here."

"Careful! About what?" Ami ranted.

Sophie stood, fascinated by those strange pale eyes darting this way and that like a frightened rabbit.

"You must be careful. *You!*" he repeated urgently, speaking directly to Sophie.

"Me?" she breathed, as an icy tingle ran down her spine.

"There's danger here…"

An angry shout echoed suddenly across the valley. "Hey you!"

The boy spun around. David Meredith was thundering towards them.

"Take great care," the boy warned as he leapt the slate wall like a gazelle. "Trust no one!"

"Why? Wait…" Sophie called, but he was gone, sprinting down into the valley like a hare running for its life.

David Meredith gave chase but eventually was forced to give up. He returned, breathless, looking like he could breathe fire.

"What did I tell you about keeping together?" he raged. "And where's the member of staff who should be at the rear making sure nothing like this could happen?"

Sophie and Ami stood quietly while he ranted on. When at last he calmed down, he demanded, "Who the devil was he anyway?"

"He didn't say. Only that…" Sophie stopped. Should she tell David Meredith of the boy's warnings? He'd said she was in danger. Yet she hadn't been in danger before coming to Wales, to Plas Dol-y-Mynydd. Therefore the danger was here, in this place. Or the danger came from someone who lived in these remote hillsides.

Someone like their instructor.

She blinked up into David Meredith's angry face. "He just wanted to know the time, that's all. His watch had stopped."

She was grateful that Ami kept her mouth shut.

Later, after dinner, she explained to Ami why she'd lied. They were sitting by the pond, watching goldfish chasing gnats on the water's surface. They spoke in whispers.

"Don't you see, Ami, if there is danger here, it must come from someone who lives or works around here."

"But what sort of danger?" Ami murmured.

Sophie let her fingers trail into the cool water. "I can only think of one thing … I keep trying not to, but it comes back, over and over again."

"The missing girl?" whispered Ami, and Sophie nodded. "Do you think that boy knows something?"

"Possibly."

"Then why didn't you tell Mr Meredith?"

Sophie lowered her voice. "Maybe our instructor knows more than anyone realizes. I bet he was here when the girl vanished last year. Maybe he had something to do with her disappearance."

"Sophie, don't!"

"We have to face it, Ami. And if that is the case and he guesses that we suspect as much – *we* could be in danger."

Ami looked sickly. "I don't think so, Sophie. Have you forgotten what the boy actually said?"

"What?"

Ami stood up. She backed away a little. "He said *you* were in danger. *You*, Sophie, no one else – just you! I think you should tell Mr Meredith. If you are in danger, he should be aware of it."

"No!" Sophie said fiercely. "If I am in some

sort of danger, it can only come from one person. And that person is David Meredith – our instructor!"

CHAPTER 6

Sophie couldn't sleep that night. She lay tossing and turning, trying to make sense of it all. Who was Helena? Was she the missing girl? But why was Sophie in danger now? What had she got to do with a girl who vanished a year ago?

Her three room-mates were fast asleep when Sophie saw the bedroom door handle turning. Her heart lurched. She lay deathly still, clutching the sheets to her chin, her heart thudding. Slowly, the door creaked open.

Miss Mooney peeped in and Sophie gave such a gasp of relief that the teacher jumped.

"Oh! I thought you'd all be asleep. I was just checking that everything was all right." She tiptoed in and sat on the edge of Sophie's bed. "What's wrong pet, can't you sleep?"

"No, miss. I keep thinking."

"Are you worried about the person outside your window last night?"

Sophie shrugged. "Yes, that, and…"

"What? What else, Sophie?"

"Something that happened today, miss."

Miss Mooney smiled kindly, and gently brushed Sophie's long red hair from her eyes. "What happened today?"

Sophie explained about the boy and his warning.

Miss Mooney listened, frowning.

"I wonder who he was. Did he say he was from the village?"

"He hardly had time to say anything," said Sophie. "He just told me to be very careful. Why, miss? Why me?"

"I've no idea," the teacher murmured. "What else did he say? You're sure he never told you his name, or where he lived?"

"No, nothing. He just said that I should be careful."

Miss Mooney gripped Sophie's wrists. The strength in the teacher's slender arms startled Sophie and as she winced in pain under the fierce grasp, Miss Mooney released her. "Sorry pet, only this is really bothering me. Look, if you see him again, I want you to tell me. Do you promise?"

Sophie was beginning to wish she hadn't mentioned it. "It's probably nothing, miss…"

"He shouldn't have frightened you, Sophie. He had no right." Her voice softened. "You'd better try and sleep, it's very late."

Sophie slid down under the blankets. "Yes. Good night, miss."

The teacher brushed a few stray red hairs from Sophie's face and tiptoed towards the door.

"Miss…"

"Yes, Sophie?"

"Don't tell Mr Meredith. I don't want him to know."

"I won't breathe a word," Mary Mooney

promised, and closed the door with a soft, final click.

When sleep finally came, Sophie was haunted by nightmares of giants. Giants as huge as the mountains. Giants with pale silvery eyes, staring down at her.

She awoke in a cold sweat, relieved that the commotion going on around her was just her friends getting dressed.

This morning, along with the usual back-packs, they were also loaded down with safety harnesses, ropes, climbing boots and hard hats.

David Meredith's mood was blacker than her own.

"…and today we stick together as a group." His black eyes bore down on Sophie. "No stragglers! You keep up! You stay alert! Do you understand?"

"Yes, Mr Meredith," answered twelve wide-eyed would-be rock climbers.

They set off, taking the same path through the woods. But while all her friends were chatting excitedly, Sophie found herself peering through the trees, to where someone might be hiding, watching. Someone with silver eyes and the agility of a gazelle.

She felt jittery, uneasy. Perhaps it had been that boy outside their window the other night. Perhaps he thought she was this Helena person. His words returned, ringing in her ears. There's danger here … trust no one…

They were walking in single file now. Way ahead, David Meredith and Mr Granger had stopped either side of the path, talking quietly. The instructor was standing by a pile of cut logs. As he talked, he absently picked up the axe that was sticking out of the pile and began chipping away at a log.

One by one, the girls filed between the two men.

The chipping, chopping sound echoed from tree to tree, drowning out the girls' chatter. It had a rhythm to it, reminding Sophie of something.

A rhyme, yes, a rhyme, and a little dance that her grandmother had taught her years ago. When two people would make an archway with their arms and everyone else would skip underneath it. Each was caught in turn and released.

Everyone except the last person.

Oranges and lemons, say the bells of St.
Clements.
You owe me five farthings, say the bells of
St. Martins.
When will you pay me, say the bells of
Old Bailey.
When I grow rich, say the bells of
Shoreditch.
When will that be, say the bells of Stepney.
I do not know, say the great bells of Bow.
Here comes the candle to light you to bed.
Here comes the chopper to chop off your
head!
Chop, chop, the last one's dead!

The words spun through her mind, echoing with every step she took. Nearer and nearer she went to David Meredith.

Chop, chop, the last one's dead!

"Sophie! Stop dawdling, you're last again," David Meredith called.

The last one's dead!

She felt sick. Dizzy. They were going to catch her between them.

Catch her and… She turned. She couldn't go on, couldn't walk between them. Couldn't.

Her legs began to move, a jerky, nervous walk back from where she'd come. Her step quickened until she was almost running. She had to get away…

Then she began to run in earnest. Faster … faster … her breath hot in her throat, her heart hammering.

The chipping, chopping sound ringing in her ears… Chop, chop, the last one's dead!

The narrow footpath twisted and turned, becoming lost to her panic-stricken eyes. Now it was nettles and brambles, and tree roots that leapt out of the earth to trip her. Branches that clawed at her clothes and hair.

Here comes the chopper to chop off your head,
Chop, chop, the last one's dead!

"Sophie!"

Danger! Trust no one!

"Sophie?"

Footsteps thudded behind her. Heavy footsteps pounding the earth, sending vibrations through her body. Footsteps getting nearer, nearer... She felt sick. Couldn't breathe... Then two powerful arms encircled her waist and she fell headlong. She tasted the damp cool earth on her lips.

CHAPTER 7

"Let me go!" Sophie cried, struggling to her feet. "Let me go!"

David Meredith pulled her to her feet, his eyes black and narrowed. His grip was like iron. Sophie was no match for his strength and she found herself wondering if this was what had happened to the missing girl?

And then, thankfully, she heard another voice. Mr Granger's voice. Breathlessly he demanded, "Meredith ... what's happened? Is she all right? Sophie, whatever's the matter? What the devil are you running away for?"

David Meredith released her and stood, arms folded, glaring down at her. "Yes, that's what I'd like to know too. Well, young lady, what have you to say for yourself?"

As her panic subsided, Sophie began to feel stupid. "I … I forgot something," she lied.

David Meredith glowered. "Then why not just say so, without all the dramatics?"

"There was no dramatics. I thought if I ran I wouldn't hold you all up."

To her surprise, David Meredith actually looked as if he believed her.

"Well, come on then, I'll take you back to the house. You're heading in the wrong direction anyhow."

"No!" she cried, and then as his expression hardened, she forced a feeble smile. "Er, just point me in the right direction."

"You'll never find it," Meredith insisted, taking her elbow.

"I will," she promised, panic widening her eyes. She couldn't allow herself to be alone with David Meredith. It was too dangerous.

"I'll go with her," said Paul Granger.

Sophie jumped at the offer. "You will? Oh thanks, that's great." And she grabbed his sleeve and pulled him away – as far away as possible from the instructor.

When they were out of earshot, Paul Granger said, "Why does he frighten you, Sophie?"

She laughed nervously. "Mr Meredith? He doesn't frighten me at all. Whatever gave you that idea?"

"A person wouldn't have to be a Sherlock Holmes to see that you were panic-stricken back there. What did he say to you?"

"Nothing."

"Has he touched you? Or hurt you?"

"No."

"Threatened you?"

"No, nothing. Honestly. It's just…"

Paul Granger halted as they reached the clearing and Dol-y-Mynydd house loomed straight ahead.

"What is it, Sophie? Look, I know I'm a bit of a newcomer to the school, and you don't know me very well, but believe me, if you've a problem, you can come to me. You can trust me, Sophie."

Trust no one.

A tiny voice echoed through her mind. Trust no one, that's what the boy had warned.

But he couldn't have meant Mr Granger, her games teacher.

On an impulse, Sophie explained all about the boy with silver eyes and his warnings. Paul Granger listened intently.

"It sounds as if the boy knows something."

"To do with the girl that vanished?"

"It's possible. Though probably he was just a crank. Or maybe a lad with an eye for a pretty girl and a novel chat-up line."

Sophie pulled a face. "Well it's certainly original."

"Go on, nip in and fetch whatever it is you forgot. But hurry, they'll be miles ahead by now."

In fact, the rest of the class were exactly where they had left them when Sophie and Mr Granger returned. A few of the girls were sitting on the freshly cut pile of logs, waiting.

A round of applause went up as Sophie and Mr Granger reappeared.

"And about time too!" said Ami reproach-fully. "I'd given you up for dead."

"Pull another stunt like that, young lady," growled David Meredith, standing just behind her, "and you'll wish you were."

CHAPTER 8

The rock they were to climb looked like a mountain, although nothing in comparison with the snowy peaked mountains in the distance.

Shielding her eyes against the sun's glare, Sophie watched David Meredith scale effortlessly to the summit, like a fly on a wall.

They had spent the last hour talking about climbing. The do's and the don'ts. What was safe and what wasn't.

"Do precisely what I tell you and you'll come to no harm," David Meredith instructed them before he began his climb. "You'll each be harnessed to a safety rope which I'll anchor at the summit. A second rope will attach you to me."

"I am not looking forward to this," Sophie confided to her best friend.

"Where's your sense of adventure?" Ami asked eagerly.

"I can't help it. I just don't like heights."

David Meredith had reached the peak and was hammering the anchorage point into the rock. At the foot of the rock face Mr Granger and the Headmaster worked together, double checking each climber's ropes and harness.

One by one, the girls scrambled, scratched or were dragged up the rock face. Finally the only ones left were the teachers and Sophie.

"Come along, Sophie," said the Head. "You've been so polite allowing all your friends to go up before you. Anyone would think you didn't want to go up at all."

"I don't," groaned Sophie.

Miss Mooney clipped the rope to her own harness, checking straps, and then pulled on the ropes. "Sophie pet, I'm useless at climbing too. I absolutely hate heights. But if I can do it, anyone can." She waved up to the instructor. "OK, David, I'm ready."

For someone who was useless at climbing, Mary Mooney scrambled up the rocks like a mountain goat. Within minutes she had disappeared over the edge of the summit. She instantly reappeared, smiling and waving.

"Easy! Come on, Sophie!"

Sophie held back, growing more nervous by the second.

"Come along, Sophie," urged the Head. "You've nothing to worry about with Mr Meredith at the top."

That's what worries me, Sophie thought to herself.

Mr Granger seemed to read her mind. He leant towards her and whispered, "Would you like me to go up before you? Then I can help him hold on to the rope – just in case."

Sophie nodded. "I'd feel happier if you were up there too."

He winked and set off, picking his way

awkwardly up the steep slope.

For a games teacher his movements were clumsy and awkward. Not that she could talk. At least he was having a go.

"Just you and me now, Sophie," said the Head as they shielded their eyes to watch Mr Granger's ascent. "I meant to speak to you earlier. Have you had any more trouble with that lad who accosted you yesterday?"

"No, I haven't seen him since."

"Good. I expect he was just a lad from the village."

"Is there a village near here then, sir?"

"Oh, yes, about a couple of miles north of Dol-y-Mynydd house I believe. Ah, he's up. Well, it looks like it's your turn now. Let's get you harnessed up."

Fastened securely in straps and ropes, Sophie reluctantly began to climb. "This is safe, isn't it, sir?"

"Safe as houses. Go on, up you go."

She didn't feel terribly safe as she inched her way from one foot hole to another, her nails digging into the rock, practically gouging out fingerholes to cling on to. Every muscle in her body tensed, her senses acute.

"Don't look down," David Meredith called.

"I've no intention of looking down," Sophie muttered to herself. She didn't need to. She could already feel the ground was a long way beneath her.

She climbed on, her leg muscles becoming so tight, they began to tremble.

The trembling spread rapidly. Within minutes they weren't like legs at all. They were two useless lumps of jelly that wouldn't carry her another inch.

She clung to the rock, eyes squeezed shut, trembling all over. A cold wind howled around her ears, chilling her bones.

"Sophie, keep moving," called David Meredith from high above her.

"Come on, Sophie, you've almost made it," shouted Mr Granger.

"I can't," she croaked, glancing down, hoping she hadn't come too far to go back. But the ground seemed a hundred miles away. The Headmaster looked like an ant. There was nothing below but rock and a whole lot of fresh air.

She felt dizzy. She started to sway. Her fingers began to loosen their grip on the rock. A hot black swampy feeling crawled over her head.

Don't faint… Don't faint…

Above her, people were yelling, shouting advice… "Sophie, don't look down. Hang on, Sophie. Sophie, be careful."

And then one voice shrieking above all the hubbub and commotion. Ami's voice. Ami – hysterical. "The rope!" Ami was screaming. "The rope! It's come off the anchorage point. Mr Meredith, don't let go, you're the only one holding her!"

The black swampy feeling closed over Sophie's head and as her fingernails scraped one final time against the rock, she felt herself falling. Falling… Falling…

CHAPTER 9

A violent jerk jolted Sophie abruptly back to consciousness.

She blinked, still dizzy, as the world came into a blurred spinning focus.

She was dangling by a single rope in mid-air. Nothing solid below, nothing solid above. No strength in her arms and legs.

Just hanging there. Like a puppet on a string.

She became aware of movement. Very slowly, she was being hauled upwards. Higher, higher. The earth a million miles below, a blue, blue sky above. Then hands reaching down, trying to grab her.

Sophie saw large suntanned hands gripping the rope, the only thing stopping her from plummeting to the ground far below.

David Meredith's hands.

The rope was cutting deep into his flesh. She looked up helplessly into his face as she hung there. The veins in his neck and forehead stood out. Sweat trickled down his cheeks. His face was contorted with pain and effort.

And then Paul Granger's hands reached her. He grabbed her harness and helped haul her up on to solid ground. Everyone crowded around as she staggered shakily to her feet.

As she got her breath, Sophie looked around for David Meredith, who had stood back as her friends crowded round.

"Yes, I'm fine, I'm OK," she told everyone. She spotted the instructor, kneeling by the anchorage point, examining it.

Paul Granger crouched down beside him. "What happened, Meredith?"

"I wish I knew. I secured this rope myself. I can't understand how it came undone."

"Good job you didn't loosen your grip then," Paul Granger added in a tight voice.

David Meredith wiped the sweat from his eyes. "Thank God Ami noticed it had come undone." He looked up and saw Sophie standing there. "Are you all right, Sophie?"

"Yes, just a bit shaky," she answered, intrigued at the intense way Paul Granger was examining the climbing gear, looking more and more puzzled. "Thank you for hanging on to me…"

"Ami's the one you ought to be thanking."

"Yes," Sophie murmured absently, worried by the look on Paul Granger's face, and alarmed suddenly by the look of hatred he cast towards the instructor.

"Are you sure you're all right?" David Meredith was asking.

"Yes … yes. Thank you. You saved my life. I'm very grateful…" her voice trailed away. And she wondered suddenly if she should be thanking the instructor at all.

Did he really save her life? Or did he come dangerously close to taking it?

CHAPTER 10

The rest of the day was disastrous. While everyone tried to act normal and pretend nothing had happened, everyone was nervy and on edge.

As for the instructor, his dark hawk-like eyes followed Sophie's every move. And was it her imagination, or was Paul Granger watching him?

Neither would let her out of their sight. It was beginning to get on her nerves.

"I just wish they'd stop watching me," she complained to Ami as they headed back to Plas Dol-y-Mynydd house.

"I suppose they both feel responsible for

you," remarked Ami as she bit into an apple. "I mean, how would they explain it to your parents if they'd had to scrape you up off the ground?"

"Shut up, Ami, I go cold every time I think about it."

"He saved your life, Sophie," Ami remarked. "You should have seen him hanging on to that rope for grim death. Wow, those muscles!"

Sophie glanced over her shoulder at David Meredith, who was walking just a few yards behind. She lowered her voice. "Ami, do you think it's possible that he didn't fasten that rope properly on purpose?"

"It's possible, I suppose," mused Ami. "Hardly likely though. I mean, why arrange for you to fall and then save you? Seems daft to me."

Sophie shrugged. "Maybe he chickened out?"

"Or," said Ami, her eyes widening, "because he knew he'd get the blame. Or better still, everyone saw how he saved you, so if something nasty was to happen to you…"

"Ami!"

"I'm only supposing. As I was saying, if something does happen … no one will think it was him, because they've all seen him saving your life before."

Sophie groaned. "I wish I'd never asked."

Ami threw an arm around Sophie's shoulder and laughed. "Stop worrying. I'm only teasing. If there is a villain around here, I'd put money on it being that nutter with the silvery eyes. Now he was creepy."

"Ami."

"Yes?"

"Do me a favour."

"Anything. What?"

"Shut up, will you!"

Ami grinned. "OK. Let's talk about food. I wonder what's for supper."

A fine grey spiral of smoke was puffing out of the tall chimney when they reached Dol-y-Mynydd house. But Sophie couldn't eat a thing. It had been an awful day.

I should have stayed in bed! she thought as she pushed her food around her plate.

Her thoughts strayed. Had that missing girl sat here like this? Maybe at this very table? Had she been warned of danger? Had she sensed something, some danger, just as Sophie did herself?

David Meredith was watching her. He looked as if he was eating. But he was watching her. And Mr Granger, watching too. Everyone, watching, watching.

The room was hot and stuffy. There was a roaring log fire, crackling and spitting in the huge grate. The heat was almost unbearable.

She scraped back her chair. "You can finish my supper, Ami. I'm not hungry."

"Where are you going?"

She was about to say that she was going for a walk, but she sensed a stillness settle over David Meredith, as if he were listening, and so she shrugged and said, "Just the bathroom."

The air outside was cool and fresh. Sophie breathed deeply as she strolled across the lawns. She sat for a while by the pond, fascinated by the fish feasting on the gnats that skimmed the surface.

The red-black sky was filled with flocks of birds flying back to the woods for the night, their high-pitched cries filling the silence.

It's lovely here, Sophie thought. If only I didn't feel so uneasy. A sudden movement amongst the trees startled her. The shadows were already lengthening, turning elm trees into gnarled old men again. But one black shape wasn't just her imagination.

It was a man, or a boy. Standing, half hidden amongst the trees. Watching her.

Sophie jumped to her feet, an icy shiver running down her spine. Run! A voice in her head screamed. Stay calm. It's nothing, she reasoned. Just someone out for a walk.

But before she could do anything, he made his move.

CHAPTER 11

"Over here!"

Sophie peered through the darkness, her fear vanishing. Instead, her heart gave a little leap.

"You!"

The boy with silver eyes!

He beckoned her to join him at the edge of the woods. Sophie hesitated. There was no one else around. Everyone was still at supper. But he looked nervous. Afraid to come out of the shadows. Afraid to be seen.

Taking a deep breath, she walked towards him. Towards those strange luminous eyes. Here in the twilight he looked unreal. Ghostly.

She stopped a short distance away from him, unwilling to enter the black canopy of trees. "What do you want?"

"I have to talk to you … to warn you."

Sophie groaned. "Don't tell me, I'm still in danger. Well unless you explain, you can just shut up. You're really spoiling this holiday for me, you know."

"I'm sorry. But it's for your own good. I'm worried about you."

Sophie folded her arms. "You don't even know me."

He looked nervous, as if someone was going to jump out on him at any minute. "I *thought* I knew you. I thought you were her."

"Who? Who did you think I was?"

"Helena, of course. I've been watching. I always watch. Hoping she'll come back to me one day."

"You're talking in riddles," Sophie said impatiently.

He shrank back into the shadows. "Come on, this way, and I'll explain everything. We don't want to be seen."

"Who are you afraid of?"

"Helena, come on, we'll be seen…"

"You called me Helena. My name's Sophie."

His silver eyes sparkled. "Did I?"

She backed away from him. Wishing now she hadn't come so far from the house. "My … my friend will be looking for me."

He stepped forward and gripped her wrist, and she gave a startled cry.

"Please, wait," he begged. "I must talk to you. I'm worried about you. You have to be careful. Be on your guard. Don't trust anyone."

"Does that include you?" asked Sophie, meeting those silvery pale eyes.

He looked confused, then glanced down at her wrist. He released her. "Sorry. Look, if I explain everything you'll understand why I'm so worried about your safety."

"That would be a good idea," she said coolly. "But if you think I'm going into the woods with you, forget it."

"OK, I'll tell you now, but if anyone comes,

I'm off." He took a deep breath. "My name's Gareth, Gareth Jones. I live in the village with my gran. Last year I met a lovely girl. She'd come here on a school trip."

"Helena?"

He nodded. "You look just like her."

"So that's why you called me Helena?"

He nodded. "She used to sneak off to meet me. It used to drive the instructor wild. He didn't like being disobeyed."

"No, I don't suppose he did."

"Anyway, on the very last day of her holiday, she didn't meet me like we arranged. I never saw her again – no one ever saw her again." His voice trembled. "I keep watching, hoping one day she'll return…"

Sophie touched his hand. "Gareth, I think you'll have to accept the fact that she may never come back."

"I know," he murmured sadly. "My gran says she's dead, and she's never wrong. She has the gift, see."

"What gift?" puzzled Sophie.

"The gift of second sight. No, don't laugh,

she's brilliant at telling fortunes and astrology and stuff. Folk in the village rely on her predictions for just about everything. They come up to the cottage so's she can read their palms, or teacups."

"Weird!"

"When I told her I thought I'd seen Helena, she read my teacup. She said it wasn't Helena, just someone like her." He hesitated. "That's when she saw the danger all around you."

Sophie shook her head. "So you think I'm in danger just because of some hocus pocus teacup reading!"

"My gran is never wrong, Sophie," he said earnestly. "If she sees danger looming, then danger's looming. Believe me!"

Sophie folded her arms. "If your gran's never wrong, how come you thought I was Helena? Your gran says she's dead."

He looked helpless and Sophie instantly regretted her outburst.

"I'm sorry…"

"No, I understand what you're saying. It's

just that I keep hoping, searching…"

"Where do you search? Surely the police have looked everywhere."

"Not everywhere," he said, looking towards the mountains.

"You think she's lost in the mountains?" breathed Sophie.

"It's the only place she can be. So I keep looking."

Sophie shook her head. "But that will take for ever – just look at that mountain range!"

He shrugged vaguely. "Then I'll search for ever."

"Oh, Gareth!" Sophie cried, feeling so sorry for him.

He brightened. "Don't look so upset. I've a system, see…" He took a piece of paper from his pocket and unfolded it. It was a sketch of the mountain range, each area numbered. A list showed where he had already looked, and where he would look next. "See, this rock is next on my list. It's full of caves and crevices. You can see it from here, look…"

He pointed far off into the distance, to a

rugged mountain of grey, streaked and pitted with black cavities.

Sophie touched his hand. "Gareth, do you really expect to find her alive?"

Sadly he shook his head.

"Sophie! Soph, is that you?"

They both turned. Ami was waving from the top of the steps.

"I have to go!" Gareth said urgently.

"No! Wait! It's only my friend."

"Take care," he said, before racing off.

Only then did she realize she was still clutching his sketch map of the mountains. She called frantically. "Gareth … your map!" But he was gone, sprinting through the woods like a startled deer.

With a sigh, Sophie dragged herself back towards the house and Ami.

"Who were you talking to?" Ami asked, running down the steps.

"Gareth. You know, the boy with the eyes."

Ami pulled a face. "Not again! What did he want?"

"It seems I look like Helena, the missing

girl. His gran is a whizz-kid with the tea leaves and she reckons I'm in danger."

"Told you he was a nutter," Ami remarked with a smug toss of her head.

"I don't think he is," murmured Sophie. "I feel sorry for him."

"Why?"

"Because he's still searching for Helena. I don't think he'll rest until she's found – one way or another. Oh, and I've got his map. I'll have to go after him; he needs this."

"Oh, Soph! Don't get involved."

Sophie looked steadily into her friend's worried face. "Ami, I *am* involved. Somehow I'm involved in this mystery. I don't know why, but one way or another I'm going to get to the bottom of it."

Ami gripped Sophie's arm. There was fear in her eyes. Gravely she said, "Sophie, you be careful. Very careful."

CHAPTER 12

By morning Sophie had made up her mind to go to the village and try and find Gareth. He needed this map, and a chat with his gran might prove interesting too!

Quietly, Sophie told Ami of her plans.

"Sophie, we've got pony trekking today."

Good," Sophie said determinedly. "I won't have to walk to the village then. I'll ride."

"Don't be stupid, Sophie. They're not going to let us go off on our own, are they."

"I'm not planning on broadcasting it," Sophie replied.

"So how do you intend giving hawk-eyed Meredith the slip?"

Sophie shrugged. "I'm not sure yet. I'll need an Ordnance Survey map to find out where the village is, anyway. Mr Granger might have one…"

In fact, Paul Granger was happy to lend her his. "This is a good one, Sophie, it shows every little nook and cranny. Is there something you particularly wanted to see?"

She forced a smile. "Not really, I'm just interested in this area. Er … there's a village nearby, isn't there?"

"Yes, it's not far as the crow flies, here…" He took the map and spread it over a table. "There! Cutting straight across the hills you could walk it in an hour or so. By road it would take you twice as long."

"Could I borrow this, please? Ami and I were discussing the height of the mountains round here, and this shows all that sort of thing, doesn't it?"

"It shows everything," he said, refolding the map for her. "Sophie, is everything OK now? Nothing's troubling you … no one's troubling you?"

"No, everything's fine," she answered brightly.

He smiled. "Good. Because you know I'm here if you need me."

Ami was waiting for her by the pond. "You got one!"

Sophie knelt on the stone slabs and spread out the map. "The village is about an hour's walk away. By horse I should be able to do it in twenty minutes."

"Don't you mean *we* can do it?"

"No, I've been thinking, Ami. You'll have to stay here and cover for me."

"How?"

Refolding the map as she wanted it, Sophie explained her plan.

"It's simple. We'll see how the teachers are situated when we set off. Then you casually mention to whoever's at the front that I'm with the teacher at the back, and vice versa."

Ami's eyebrows arched. "You make it sound so easy."

"It's important, Ami. I have to go and find Gareth."

It was mid-morning by the time they reached the stables. All the ponies were out grazing in a meadow. They varied in size from an enormous white shire, to one not much bigger than a Shetland pony.

Sophie instantly spotted the one she wanted. A frisky brown stallion that trotted up and down the perimeters of the meadow while the others seemed content just to graze.

He looked alert, lively, ready to gallop across the hills and dales. He would fly like the wind. She would be at the village and back before anyone even missed her.

A rosy-cheeked young woman in riding breeches and aran sweater joined them. "We'll get them saddled up and ready then," she announced. "Have any of you ever ridden before?"

Sophie's hand was up in a flash.

"Only one of you! So who, I wonder, is going to get Everest?" She flashed dark laughing eyes at David Meredith. "Looks like you again, David."

"Everest and I are old friends," he said,

casting a huge white smile at the pretty Welsh stable girl. Mary Mooney's face registered her disapproval.

Ami gave Sophie a nudge. "Mooning Mary's got a touch of the green-eyed monster. Just look at her, she's seething."

Sophie wasn't listening. "Could I ride the brown stallion, please?"

The stable girl eyed Sophie critically. "He's a lively one. Do you think you can handle him?"

"Oh, yes, I have ridden before."

"Don't worry, I'll be keeping an eye on her," said David Meredith.

Sophie gritted her teeth. That was the last thing she wanted. She would have to prove that she was a capable horse rider.

The opportunity arose as they were all saddling up. Ami was struggling with the bridle and bit. "I don't like the way this horse is looking at me. Open your mouth, you stupid creature, and put this in."

Sophie had finished saddling Satin, her pony. She turned her hand to helping Ami with the shorter and sturdier piebald.

"Ami, listen, I want you to keep our instructor occupied."

"Oh, and how exactly do I do that?"

Sophie grinned. "Just make him think you're totally useless with horses. Shouldn't be too hard!"

"Thanks!"

"He'll have to watch you, to make sure you don't fall off."

"While you're galloping off into the sunset."

"I have to!"

Miss Mooney came up behind her and tugged at Sophie's long red hair. "Sophie, why don't you tuck this under your riding cap? If it catches in a branch while you're trotting along it could be very nasty."

"I don't think it will all tuck in, miss, but I'll plait it."

Mary Mooney's attention switched abruptly to David Meredith, who was heading towards them, leading the enormous Everest. "Ah, David! I think I'm going to need a helping hand to get on to my pony."

81

"I'll be with you in two minutes, Mary," he said distractedly, examining the saddles on Sophie and Ami's horses. They were both faultless. His eyebrows rose. "Excellent."

"Don't look at me, Mr Meredith," said Ami. "Sophie did it all, she's the expert. As for me, I'm going to need all the help I can get."

"David…" Mary Mooney called, as she struggled to make her pony stand still.

"One moment, Mary."

Sophie gave Satin's ear a gentle stroke and then swung easily into the saddle. David Meredith looked impressed. "You don't have to worry about me today, Mr Meredith," said Sophie. "I love horses and I'm a very competent rider. I've a room full of rosettes at home."

"I believe you," he remarked, turning to Ami. She cast him a helplessly sickly smile.

"Anyone got a stepladder?" she asked impishly.

They eventually got underway. It felt good to be back in the saddle. Sophie had always loved riding. And Satin was a beautiful pony, responding willingly to each command. As for Ami, Sophie couldn't tell if she was really as bad a horsewoman as she looked, or if she was overacting for their instructor's benefit.

They headed up into the hills, where the wind blew up from the moors, and where little streams and brooks criss-crossed and a hundred different mosses and ferns coloured the earth. After an hour or so they stopped for lunch. Ami had to be lifted down off her pony by the instructor – much to everyone's amusement. Mary Mooney remained saddled until Paul Granger came to her assistance. But it was David Meredith that she sat beside to eat her sandwiches.

"So when's the great escape?" Ami whispered as they tucked into their packed lunches.

"As soon as we get going again," said Sophie, smoothing out the map and tracing a line with her finger. "We're following this path – it goes full circle back to the stables."

"My, quite the little map reader!" remarked Ami as she unscrewed her pop bottle.

"Just here," whispered Sophie, pointing, "is the closest we get to the village. That's when I make my break. You will cover for me, won't you?"

"No problem," Ami promised. "Trust me."

Back in the saddle, Sophie gradually allowed all the other riders to pass her. The Headmaster and Mr Granger were at the rear. There had been a panic-stricken look on the Headmaster's face since struggling up into the saddle that morning. He still looked unsure of himself, whereas Paul Granger and his young mare looked restless, as if they would enjoy a gallop across the hills too, rather than plodding along with the Headmaster.

"Enjoying yourself, sir?" asked Sophie, slowing Satin so they could catch up.

"Give me a car any day," the Headmaster complained, fidgeting uncomfortably. "I'm too broad in the beam and too long in the tooth for this kind of activity."

Sophie laughed and directed Mr Granger's attention to Miss Mooney. "I think Miss Mooney is having a spot of bother too. I'll stay and look after Sir if you want to trot on a bit."

He didn't need telling twice. He took off like the wind. Quite the expert horseman, Sophie realized.

She brought Satin into line with the Headmaster, deliberately slowing the pace, and increasing the gap between them and the rest of the group. Way ahead, David Meredith glanced back. Sophie waved cheerfully, then Ami, beside him, wobbled, and his attention was back on her.

They were close now to the point where Sophie knew she must make her move. To her right stretched hills and valleys where she could quickly dip out of sight. If only she could get away from the Headmaster for a moment.

Quite suddenly, the problem was solved for her. A fox darted out from the undergrowth and shot in front of them. Both horses reared back in fright. Sophie quickly calmed Satin but the Headmaster's horse took fright and bolted. Within seconds, he had caught up with the others and overtaken them, hanging on to the horse's neck for dear life. David Meredith and Paul Granger instantly gave chase.

Sophie made her move.

With a determined tug on the reins, she brought Satin around.

"Now, Satin, now!"

Pressed low to his velvet neck, her red plait whipping in the wind like a brilliant flame, Sophie galloped feverishly away from the chaos behind her. Towards Gareth and his gran, and maybe an answer to this mystery.

CHAPTER 13

She had made a good choice, picking Satin. His hooves pounded the moors tirelessly. She urged him on, seated low, letting the wind flow over them, frantically looking back, afraid that she would see David Meredith galloping after her. But there was no sign of him, or anyone. She galloped on, coaxing Satin to the very limits. On and on. Gradually, she slowed. She looked back less frequently, easing up on Satin, allowing him to slow to a gentle canter. Her plan had worked. All that was behind was the rolling hills and valleys. And ahead now, she glimpsed the spire of a church. And gradually old slate cottages, tiny village shops and cobbled streets.

"We've made it, Satin," Sophie breathed, patting his hot smooth neck. "Good boy. Good boy."

Satin's hooves clattered along the cobbles as they trotted into the heart of the village, passing thatched cottages with rose-strewn gardens.

Sophie searched for a post office, and found it on the village square. She dismounted and tethered Satin to a railing beneath an oak tree.

The plump postmistress smiled broadly. "Afternoon, my lovely. Is it stamps you want?"

"No, thank you. I'm looking for a friend," Sophie explained. "His name's Gareth Jones; I wondered if you knew him."

The postmistress chuckled. "We've got lots of Jones in the village. There's Jones the milkman, Jones the grocer…"

"He's about sixteen or seventeen. Tall with copper-coloured hair and very pale eyes.

Silvery eyes."

The postmistress thought for a moment. "Sounds like it could be Jones the Prophet's grandson. Them that live at the back of the cemetery."

"Jones the Prophet?"

"S'right my lovely. Old Mrs Jones is blessed with the gift, you know."

"The gift of second sight?" said Sophie knowingly.

"She's a marvel. Do you know, she told my daughter she'd be having twin girls, we was able to get everything knitted in pink before the babies were born."

"Really?" murmured Sophie, unimpressed. "Could you tell me where she lives?"

"Oh, it's not far, my lovely," the postmistress said. "Are you going for a reading yourself?"

"A reading?"

"Your palm. Amazing at reading palms she is. Or she'll work out your horoscope. She predicted the very hour that old Mrs Taylor would pass away."

Sophie smiled feebly. "Really? Could you just tell me how to find her?"

The postmistress walked her to the door. "And as for her herbal remedies, why she'll fix anything from a fever to a boil on your cat's backside."

"She sounds amazing," said Sophie flatly. "Do I go right or left?"

"Well now, let's see. You follow this lane up the hill till you get to the cemetery. There's a path running along by the church wall. Follow that till you can't get any further."

"Thank you."

"Now mind how you go. Is that your horse?"

Sophie untethered Satin. "Only for the afternoon."

"Well, you'll have to tie him by the trough, he'll not get along the path."

Sophie waved her thanks as she swung into the saddle, wondering if there was some truth in this fortune telling business after all.

Wild flowering hedgerows and brambles laden with ripe juicy blackberries lined their route as Satin's hooves clattered along the cobbled lane. At the top of the hill she found the old iron water trough, a relic from the days when everyone travelled on horseback.

"There you go, Satin," she said, stroking his ears, "fresh, clean water and dandelion leaves. I won't be long."

Sophie walked briskly along the footpath by the churchyard wall. Tall ferns and nettles stood waist high, keeping her to the narrow little track. Overhead, a leafy canopy blocked out the sun and brought a sudden chill to her bones.

She tried not to think of the graves just the other side of the wall. Tried desperately not to think of ghosts or skeletons or eyes watching her as she made her lonely way onwards.

Eventually she found the cottage, tucked almost out of sight amongst the trees. A riot of scents drifted on the breeze. Lavender, mint, coriander, fennel. Every type of herb. She stood for a moment, breathing in the wild aromas.

Then, a little nervously, she followed the crooked path to the door and knocked. Timidly at first, then when no answer came, louder, willing Gareth to appear. Wishing more than anything to see those strange silvery eyes looking at her again.

But no one answered her knocking.

She wandered around to the back of the house, picking her way through the tangle of herbs that grew riotously.

There was a tiny ramshackle wooden shed at the bottom of the garden.

"Hello! Hello! Is there anyone here?"

The only sound was the buzzing of honey bees flitting from one flower to the next.

"Hello…"

Her fingers closed around the shed door handle. It opened to her pull, creaking on rusty hinges.

After the bright sunshine, the shed looked black inside. One small grimy window allowed a single shaft of sunlight to penetrate the gloom.

It acted like a spotlight, drawing Sophie's

gaze to the photograph cut from an old newspaper and nailed to the wall, discoloured and curling with age.

Sophie drew nearer, squinting.

It was a photograph of a girl. A girl with long red hair like hers. With a smile like hers. With eyes and nose and mouth like hers. With a jolt, Sophie realized she could be staring at a picture of herself!

CHAPTER 14

Sophie could hardly believe her eyes.

No wonder Gareth had thought she was Helena. They were almost identical. Particularly the hair. There weren't many people who shared the same long, straight, red hair.

With growing intrigue, she read the news story, dated over a year ago.

"Fifteen-year-old Helena Bright of St. Mark's Convent has not been seen since last Friday. This picture was taken by a school friend just hours before the pretty teenager vanished. Despite an intensive search of the area, police have found no clue to her whereabouts."

Sophie read on. There were statements from her teachers and school friends. A statement from David Meredith, who was the last person to see her.

Poor Helena, Sophie thought. She looked so happy and carefree in shorts and T-shirt, her hair hanging loosely on her shoulders.

In the background of the picture stood Plas Dol-y-Mynydd house and people in climbing gear. Sophie frowned. What was it about the picture that seemed wrong?

A sound from the doorway made her swing around. A tiny figure stood there, silhouetted against the sunlight. "Helena!"

"No, I'm not Helena," Sophie said kindly, stepping out into the sunshine. "My name's Sophie. I'm looking for Gareth Jones. Does he live here?"

A small cold hand touched Sophie's arm. Bony fingers with brown, paper-like skin stretched loosely across them closed tightly around her wrist. The old woman's eyes were sunk deep into her skull, but they were bright, sharp silvery eyes which told Sophie that this was indeed Gareth's gran.

"Sophie, so you're the one! Come into the kitchen, child. Gareth's told me all about you."

The old lady's kitchen was cluttered with plants and jars, potions and bottles. Shelves piled with books on everything from ancient remedies to star gazing. Astrological charts covered the walls along with diagrams of plants and wildlife. And overall was the lingering scent of lavender and lemons.

"I understand you can tell fortunes," Sophie said as Gareth's gran filled a copper kettle and placed it on a gas ring. Carefully she set out two delicate china teacups and saucers.

"I can tell your fortune, child, or I can give you a cure for your ailments. I've a potion for headache and stomach-ache and boils and ulcers." She chuckled. "If I'd lived a couple of hundred years ago, I'd have been burnt at the stake for being a witch."

Sophie smiled uneasily, not sure whether the old lady was joking or not.

Still chuckling, the old woman shuffled

across the room and returned with a biscuit tin. "Take a biscuit child, but you're not to dunk it in your tea. Not if I'm to read your tea leaves."

"Gareth said you read tea leaves," Sophie said. "He also said that I'm in some kind of danger. I don't mean to be rude, Mrs Jones, but I don't really believe in all that kind of stuff."

The old woman said nothing, but warmed the teapot and added milk to the cups. She didn't speak again until she had poured the tea and sat down.

"Folk don't, not until it's been proven to them, one way or another," she said, her silvery eyes twinkling. "Don't worry child, you'll not offend me."

Sophie smiled.

"Now drink your tea and we'll see what the leaves have to say ... whether you believe it or not."

Sophie saw no point in arguing, and drank. As she drained her cup and saw the formation of tiny black leaves form shapes at the base of the cup, she realized her hands were trembling. An uneasy feeling was beginning to churn deep inside of her. A feeling of dread. Whatever her future held for her, she had a sinking feeling that it wasn't going to be good news.

CHAPTER 15

Bright silvery old eyes waited patiently for Sophie to set down her teacup.

Sophie was in no hurry. At last things were starting to make sense – the reason David Meredith stared at her that first night. Looking so much like Helena, he must have thought he was seeing a ghost. And now she understood why Gareth thought she was Helena too.

"Why does Gareth think I'm in danger?" Sophie asked, still clutching her empty cup.

"Listen to me, child. Gareth always hoped Helena would return, so he'd wait and look at everyone who arrived at the big house for a holiday. It broke my heart to watch him."

"Yes, I can imagine," said Sophie softly.

"But time and again, I showed him the tea leaves. They showed the poor lass lying dead."

"Where?" Sophie demanded quickly. "They've never found her body."

The old woman shook her greying head. "I can't tell. The leaves won't come clear enough. And then Gareth came home the other night so excited. Said he'd seen Helena up at Dol-y-Mynydd house. So I read his tea leaves. Sure enough there was this lovely lass with long red hair. But it wasn't his Helena."

"It was me," breathed Sophie. "Gareth thought I was her."

The old woman's face darkened. "There was something else in the tea leaves. Something sinister, like a black hand of death hanging over the red-haired lass."

A cold shiver crawled up Sophie's spine. "That's ridiculous!"

The old woman closed her wrinkled eyes for a second. "It's your own decision whether

to take heed of my warnings or not, child."
And then she fixed Sophie with a look that
chilled. "But I'd never forgive myself if I
hadn't warned you."

With trembling hands, Sophie gave the old
woman the cup and watched fascinated as she
twirled it three times before upturning it on
the saucer. She was a long while coming to
her conclusions.

Finally she put down the cup and took
Sophie's hand. "Child, take care," she said
gravely. "I wasn't mistaken. There is danger
growing all around you. Already you've come
dangerously close to death."

"What!"

"A climbing accident?"

Sophie gasped. "How do you know?"

"It's in the leaves, child," she said,
squeezing Sophie's hand. "Take care, it was
no accident. At this very moment a terrible
hatred is festering from someone close to you.
From someone you trust."

Sophie wanted to laugh it off, but she felt as
if she was being strangled.

"Who?" she croaked.

"I can't tell, child. If only I could."

"What can I do?" asked Sophie quietly.

"Don't go back there, child. Danger awaits you at Dol-y-Mynydd. Ah, I see in the leaves that you rode here. You have a horse waiting?"

"Yes."

"Then ride like the wind. Ride swiftly before it's too late."

Sophie jumped to her feet, her head spinning. She didn't want to believe all this mumbo-jumbo, but yet…

She had to see Gareth, to speak to him and of course return his map. "I need to see Gareth, Mrs Jones, is he here?"

The old woman shook her greying head. "No, child. I've not set eyes on my grandson since yesterday evening."

"Yesterday! You mean he didn't come home? Aren't you frantic?"

The old woman smiled. "There's no need for me to worry. Gareth often camps overnight. He'll be in the mountains, searching.

He'll be back shortly."

Sophie stared at her. "In the mountains, looking for Helena?"

The woman nodded sadly. "He'll not give up until she's found. I pray it's soon." She took Sophie's hand. "But it's you we have to worry about now. Remember child, take care. Great care. Trust no one."

Sophie left the cottage with the old woman's warning ringing in her ears.

Clouds had gathered now. Foreboding and black. Like her future. The footpath past the churchyard was uninviting. What if the danger had followed her here? Lurking just beyond the churchyard wall? What if someone was hiding just behind that tree? Or crouched low in the grass? Or waiting out on the lonely hills for her?

Perhaps the old woman was crazy. Perhaps Gareth was just as mad. Maybe there was no truth in anything that either of them had said. But what if they were telling the truth? Perhaps she shouldn't return to Dol-y-Mynydd house. But what would Ami think if she didn't return? Wouldn't it be just like Helena, never seen again?

Another frightening thought struck her. What if the old woman had told Helena the same thing? Warned her not to return. Persuaded her to get away from Plas Dol-y-Mynydd. Perhaps it was the old woman's fault that Helena went missing. An awful thought struck her. What if Helena's disappearance was more sinister than she had let herself believe? What if Helena had been murdered!

What if Gareth or his grandmother had killed poor Helena? Buried her in the graveyard one dark night? Who would think of looking for a body in a graveyard?

Her head throbbed. That was ridiculous. Why would Gareth spend his life searching for her if he knew what had become of her? But what if someone else had murdered Helena? Someone like the instructor!

With an aching head, she at last emerged from the path on to the cobbled street. She ran to where she'd left Satin. Perhaps she could ride to the stables and ask the stable girl to arrange for a taxi to take her to the railway station. Maybe she could borrow the fare home.

Rounding the bend, she saw Satin standing just where she had left him.

But Satin wasn't alone.

Grazing next to him was Everest.

The instructor's horse.

CHAPTER 16

The instructor was perched on the wall watching the horses graze, arms folded, his expression grim. Sophie fought back her first instinct to run, and walked straight up to him.

"Hello, Mr Meredith. What are you doing here?"

Slowly he stood, towering over her. "I could ask you the same question," he growled. "Care to explain yourself?"

Trembling inside, she said, "I was looking for a friend of mine. I've something I must return to him."

"Have you indeed," he remarked sarcastically. "And did you find him?"

"No…" She stopped, deciding quickly not to tell David Meredith anything about Gareth or his gran.

He glanced over her head to the pathway by the churchyard. "He lives along there, does he?"

"The woman from the post office thought he might live there. But it wasn't him at all," she lied, not about to put Gareth into more danger if David Meredith was the guilty one.

David Meredith untethered both horses and slapped Satin's reins into Sophie's hand. "Is there anywhere else you'd like to look before we go back?"

"No," she murmured. There was no point in delaying the inevitable – the return journey across the lonely Welsh hillsides with a man who could already have murdered.

At least it was still light now. Any later and the sun would be going down.

"Let's go then."

Sophie swung into the saddle, amazed that he hadn't ranted and raved at her. But the awful silence seemed worse.

She soon realized he was just biding his time. Once away from the village, he let rip. "Are you aware of the trouble you've caused?"

"I didn't think I'd be missed," she argued.

"Not missed! I'm personally accountable for every child who comes here."

"Sorry."

"There was absolute panic stations back there when we realized you'd vanished. I don't suppose you had anything to do with your poor Headmaster's horse bolting like that?"

"No!" she gasped. "I wouldn't. It was a fox … I just grasped the opportunity to nip off." She hesitated. "Is the Head all right?"

"Battered and bruised, but he'll live. As for you, when I realized you'd gone, I thought…"

She turned and saw his eyes were creased in pain. "Yes?"

He heaved a sigh. "I thought history was about to be repeated. It brought back a very tragic incident. And then I questioned, or should I say interrogated, your friend Ami and she spilled the beans."

"Do the others know you've come to get me?" Sophie asked, her hopes rising. He could hardly harm her if everyone knew he'd come after her.

"You've caused an absolute uproar. I should think half of Wales knows what's happened, let alone the class."

"I'm sorry, I never meant to upset everything."

"Well you should have thought about that," he growled. "Now you'll just have to take the consequences of your actions."

"What do you mean?" she asked, suddenly fearful again.

He glanced angrily at her. "I'd be perfectly within my rights to send you straight home. You just can't be trusted."

Yes, do that! she thought. That was exactly what Gareth's grandmother had wanted. There was danger at Dol-y-Mynydd house. Yet to return home without seeing Gareth again was unthinkable. She could feel the instructor's eyes upon her. She stared straight ahead.

At last he said, "Don't you realize how easy it is to get lost in these hills?"

"I've got a map."

"What if you'd fallen and injured yourself?"

"I'm a competent rider."

"You're very sure of yourself," he remarked coolly. "You remind me of someone else who once stayed here. You look a lot like her too."

"Really. Who?" she asked nervously, knowing full well that he meant Helena.

"That doesn't matter. What does matter is the fact that like you, she was always going off doing her own thing. She was never where she was supposed to be. Always missing. She led me a merry dance trying to keep her under control. I virtually had to keep a twenty-four hour watch on the girl. Even then it wasn't enough…"

So Helena was a wilful girl who didn't like to follow orders, thought Sophie. And David Meredith was a man who didn't like to be disobeyed. Perhaps her continual disobedience had angered him and he'd hit her or something. Perhaps he'd killed her accidentally. Perhaps...

"It's getting cold, do you mind if we gallop for a while?" Sophie suggested, wishing that she could see the tall bricked chimney pots of the old house.

"What's the great rush?" he asked quietly.

They cantered on, his mount, Everest, just slightly ahead of her and Satin. The sun was low, its last rays struggling through pillows of grey cloud.

Sophie shivered. How much further? The journey seemed endless.

"We are heading the right way, aren't we?" she asked, after riding for ever and still not seeing any familiar landmarks. It hadn't taken this long to travel to the village. Surely the house ought to be in sight by now.

An odd sense of unease crawled through her.

"You're the one with the map," he remarked unkindly.

She pulled the map from her pocket and studied it. But now there were no reference points. Nothing to say where they were. No trail, no distant spire. Nothing.

Angrily Sophie turned the map upside down and studied it from another angle. Somehow they must have veered off the route she'd mapped out for herself.

They were lost. Just as he'd predicted.

He was watching her. Enjoying her growing panic. She began to feel sick. There was no one around for miles. Just her and the instructor.

Had this been his intention from the start, to get her alone, deep in the hills?

Is this what he did with poor Helena?

CHAPTER 17

Sophie didn't wait to find out. She tugged at Satin's reins, turning him around and then, pressing her heels against his warm body, she broke into a furious gallop.

"Hey!"

David Meredith's startled yell rang in her ears as they bolted away, back towards what she hoped was the village. She crouched lower over Satin's neck, urging him on. "Faster boy!"

Glancing back, she saw him thundering after her. But surely Satin could out-run the lumbering Everest. He had to.

"Come on, Satin, faster boy!"

The wind whipped his black mane into her eyes while her body tensed. Her thighs ached unbearably as she clung on to the powerful animal as they pounded across the moors.

To her fright, she heard the thud, thudding of Everest's hooves growing closer and closer behind her.

She glanced back. David Meredith was closing the distance rapidly. His face set and grim. His riding expertise far greater than hers. As for Everest, Sophie had been mistaken in believing him a great lump of a horse. Those huge muscular legs pounded along, his stamina far outweighing Satin's.

"Go, Satin, go! You mustn't stop, you mustn't!"

But the instructor was nearly upon them. Getting closer by the second. Her heart thudded in time with the hoof beats.

And then, in the distance, coming towards her, Sophie glimpsed another rider. Her heart gave a leap. David Meredith must have seen him too, for he instantly eased back. The distance between them lengthened again. As the rider came nearer, Sophie recognized Paul Granger. Never had she been so relieved to see anyone in her life. Satin was reluctant to stop, and Paul Granger had to manoeuvre his pony about to catch at her reins as she flew by.

David Meredith cantered up beside them a moment later. Steam rose from all three horses. Sophie edged closer to Mr Granger as she faced an irate David Meredith.

"What's going on?" demanded Paul Granger, eyeing Meredith suspiciously.

"Ask her," growled Meredith, his eyes glittering with rage. "This crazy pupil of yours just took it into her head to bolt off. Well, that settles it, miss, you're grounded until I can arrange for you to be sent home."

Sophie said nothing. She sat, breathing heavily. Knowing it was for the best, yet feeling wretched.

"Sophie? What have you got to say?" Paul Granger asked.

"Nothing," she said softly.

The two men continued to glare from each other to her. Finally Paul Granger suggested that the instructor lead on. When he was out of earshot, and they were heading back towards the house at a more leisurely pace, Paul Granger said quietly, "OK, so what's all this about?"

Certain that David Meredith couldn't overhear, she quietly told her teacher all about Gareth's gran and the warnings. And how she thought David Meredith had deliberately allowed her to become lost just now.

"If you hadn't come along, I don't know what would have happened," she confided, shivering at the thought.

"I thought I'd better. I knew you were nervous at being alone with Meredith. I must have missed you in the village," he explained. "You think Meredith had something to do with the girl's disappearance last year, don't you?"

"Yes … no… Oh, I don't know!"

"If only there was proof!" Paul Granger stated angrily.

Sophie frowned at him, startled by the frustration in his voice.

"Tell me *everything* he said and did, Sophie, and don't leave anything out. It might be very important."

The journey back to the house passed quickly as Sophie related everything to the teacher, including Gareth's gran and the tea leaves. Even the newspaper cutting in Gareth's shed. Yet when she had finished, she couldn't help feeling that she had missed something ... Something vital.

They were closer to the house than she realized and before long they trotted into the grounds.

David Meredith instructed them both to dismount. "I'll take all the horses back to the stables," he said abruptly. "You, young lady, had better report to your Headmaster."

Sophie said nothing, but dismounted and handed Satin's reins to the instructor.

All the girls rushed out, surrounding her, eager to know what had happened. But Sophie didn't feel like talking and was relieved when the Head dispersed them.

When they were alone, he took her to one

side. "I can't believe this of you, Sophie. What have you got to say for yourself?"

"I was just looking for a friend."

"Then you should have told us. If you needed to go into the village that badly, I would have accompanied you."

"Sorry, sir."

"Poor Mr Meredith had to go looking for you. You've had us all worried to death…"

"Is she all right?" Mary Mooney called as she came running across the lawns. "Sophie, where did you go?"

"Into the village, miss."

"But why?"

"I was looking for Gareth."

"Who exactly is this Gareth person, anyway?" demanded the Head.

Sophie raised her troubled eyes. "A local lad who used to know Helena Bright."

"Where does he live, Sophie?" asked Miss Mooney.

But before Sophie could reply, the Head asked irritatedly, "And who on earth is Helena Bright? Would somebody kindly tell me what's going on?"

"She's the girl who vanished from here last year," explained Sophie. The Headmaster's face dropped.

Mary Mooney put her arm around Sophie's shoulders and spoke kindly. "Headmaster, I think Sophie's had enough for one day. Let me take her in and see if cook's saved her any dinner."

"Yes, go on then," said the Head, dismissing them with a wave of his hand. "Where's Mr Granger? I want a word with him."

"I'm being sent home," Sophie said miserably as she and Miss Mooney trudged up the big stone steps.

Miss Mooney looked outraged. "Oh, that's grossly unfair. I'll speak to the Head."

"It wasn't him, it was David Meredith."

"Then I'll have a word with him. Where is he?"

"He's taking the horses back to the stables."

Miss Mooney was silent a moment, then she murmured a soft "Oh!"

"I don't suppose he'll be long," Sophie added, guessing that Mary Mooney wasn't too thrilled at David Meredith being alone with the pretty stable maid. Poor Miss Mooney, she was so plain. And it was quite obvious that she fancied the instructor. Obviously, she didn't think him capable of murder!

Sophie felt wretched. She'd spoiled everyone's day. Even Mary Mooney's.

It was late when the instructor returned. Everyone was in the main dayroom. Some of the girls were playing table tennis, some reading, others listening to walkmans. The teachers were grouped together playing cards.

Everyone looked up when David Meredith entered. Without a word to anyone, he strode through to the kitchen to make himself a coffee.

Ami and Sophie were perched together on a window seat, discussing the possibilities of what had happened to Helena.

Ami whispered, "What's his method then,

Sophie? Strangulation? A dagger through the heart? Or does he just glare at his victims with those black eyes of his and turn them into stone?" She giggled.

"It's no joke, Ami, I was really scared out there on those hills with him."

Ami became serious. "You know something, I think it would be for the best if you did go home. This place has unnerved you. Now I'm not saying you're paranoid but…"

"Thanks!" Sophie got up and headed for the door.

David Meredith barred her exit. "Going somewhere?"

"Yes, my room," she replied, embarrassed. Everyone was watching, waiting to see if he would allow her to go, or make her stay where he could see her, like a naughty child.

Mary Mooney came to her rescue. "David, can we talk?"

But the instructor paid her no attention and Sophie felt sorry for Miss Mooney, who was beginning to turn pink.

David Meredith spoke softly, so that only

those close to him could hear. "Your room and nowhere else. I'll be checking. And don't forget, you're grounded, until I decide what to do with you."

"You're sending me home," Sophie reminded him unhappily.

He didn't answer at first. Then, "You'll be the first person I've ever had to do that with. I'll sleep on it."

Despite everything, Sophie felt ridiculously glad. To be sent home would bring shame on her school. Not to mention what her parents would say. Perhaps Ami was right, maybe she was paranoid. Maybe Helena had just run away. Maybe she was still alive somewhere.

It was only when Mary Mooney turned her back and stalked off that the instructor realized she had been trying to gain his attention. He called after her. "Sorry, Mary, did you want me?"

Sophie escaped to her room. Poor Mary Mooney, *of course* she wanted him. But he was too preoccupied with her even to notice Mary.

As she got ready for bed, Sophie felt quite sorry for her teacher.

She was still wide awake and feeling guilty about Miss Mooney when Jenny and Joanne came to bed.

"Jenny, is it true that Mary Mooney was engaged once?"

"I think so."

"What happened?"

"Her fiancé went off with a younger woman as far as I know," Jenny replied as she peeled her socks off and stuffed them into her boots.

"It broke her heart," chipped in Joanne. "I overheard her telling someone not long after she started at our school. "Oh, I remember, it was at our last Christmas concert. She said the other woman was younger and very beautiful with…"

A sharp rat-a-tat sound at their door broke off the conversation. David Meredith looked in.

"Just checking," he said, looking directly at Sophie. "Remember, you're grounded. You don't set foot out of this house without my permission."

"Can't she go canoeing, sir?" begged Jenny.

"No!" came the abrupt reply. And the door and the subject were firmly closed.

With a sigh, Sophie pulled the blankets around her neck and tried to sleep.

CHAPTER 18

A bright, clear morning greeted them. The sun was shining and not a breath of wind stirred the leaves.

A perfect day for canoeing on the lake.

Sophie sat on the stone steps and watched enviously as everybody prepared for their day out.

Mary Mooney sat down beside her and stroked the stray red hairs from Sophie's face. "Sorry, Sophie, I did try and persuade Mr Meredith to change his mind. But he was adamant."

Ami joined them. "Poor old Soph! Fancy being stuck here, all alone on such a glorious day."

With her elbows on her knees and chin in hands, Sophie said nothing.

David Meredith strode across the lawns and stood before all three, legs apart, thumbs tucked down his belt, looking powerful and determined. Ignoring the smile Mary Mooney flashed at him, he glowered down at Sophie and said, "Don't forget, miss, you're grounded."

Sophie nodded.

"Right, everyone into the Land Rovers. Mary, you can drive, can't you?"

"Well, yes, but I thought I'd sit with you. The Headmaster can take the other vehi—"

"Let him drive if you like, but I want Paul Granger with me. I need to talk to the man."

Poor Miss Mooney, Sophie thought, as she saw the look of disappointment on her plain face.

Sadly, Sophie walked with everyone to the vehicles and watched quietly as they piled into the Land Rovers that were laden with canoes strapped to roof racks and trailers.

" 'Bye, Soph!" Ami called miserably from one window. "Chin up!"

Sophie attempted a smile and a wave as the Land Rovers' wheels churned up great clouds of dust and they growled off down the lane. She stood watching dejectedly until they were out of sight and the dust had settled.

Silence settled over the old house.

After a moment she could hear the birds chirping and the sheep bleating in far off meadows again. With a sigh, she wandered over to the pond and sat for a long while watching the fish and newts, lost in thought.

It was strange that Gareth hadn't been back for his map. He must have missed it by now, and surely he would remember that he'd last shown it to her. It was odd too that he hadn't returned home the other night.

A shiver ran through her suddenly. Gareth *was* all right, wasn't he?

Angry with herself, she got to her feet and marched down to the woods. Stop it! She told herself. Of course Gareth was all right. What was happening to her? She was becoming paranoid!

For a while, Sophie enjoyed the sights and

sounds of the thicket, occasionally catching sight of a squirrel and once even a fox.

Wandering back to the house, she heard someone call her name. The cook was calling to her from the steps.

"You're Sophie, aren't you?"

"Yes."

"Telephone, quickly now. Sounds urgent."

"A phone call? For me?"

Gareth! It had to be. Sophie raced across the lawns and into the house.

The phone in the corridor was dangling from its cord. "Hello? Sophie speaking. Is that you G—"

"Things have changed…" It was a woman's voice.

"Who is this?" asked Sophie, puzzled, trying to put a name to the familiar voice.

"It's me, Gareth's gran."

"Oh, hello, Mrs Jones. What's changed?"

"*Things* have changed," she repeated, her voice rising.

"What things?"

"The leaves … the tea leaves."

"Calm down, Mrs Jones. Tell me what's wrong."

The old woman only spoke more rapidly. "I thought he was all right, Gareth. But when he didn't come home again last night, I got to worrying. This morning I read my tea cup and saw that things are bad. Gareth's in trouble. I know it, I know it for certain!"

"What kind of trouble?" Sophie asked, a horrible buzzing sensation in her head.

The woman was panicking, fear quivering her old, cracked voice. "I don't know, Sophie, that's the worst of it. I don't know."

"Please, Mrs Jones, please try and keep calm," Sophie begged, shivering despite the warmth of the sun that glinted in through the windows.

"He's hurt. I can see him lying on a ridge, high up somewhere. In the mountains I think. He needs help, I know he needs help."

"Don't you worry, Mrs Jones, I'll go and look for him."

"I'm getting some of my neighbours to form a search party. The village bobby has always believed in my predictions. He's organizing the search."

"Good. Now don't worry. I'm sure Gareth will be all right. Please try not to worry too much. I'll speak to you soon."

Sophie hung up. There was nothing else for it, she had to disobey David Meredith's orders.

Gareth was in trouble.

Hastily she scribbled a note and pinned it to the outside of her bedroom door before dashing outside. Despite the sunshine, she felt like ice.

If she could find Gareth at all, would she find him alive and well?

Or dead?

CHAPTER 19

Thinking quickly, Sophie dug out Gareth's sketched map of the mountains from her jeans pocket, and then went in search of some form of transport that would be quicker than walking.

There were some bicycles in a shed. She sorted out one that had its tyres up and hastily wheeled it out into the open.

Within minutes, she was pedalling like crazy. Through the woods, out across the hills, towards the mountainous ridges in the distance, and, in particular, the one Gareth had pointed out to her. The one he planned on searching next.

As she cycled on, heading directly towards the great grey craggy wall pitted with black foreboding caves and cavities, she hoped and prayed that she would find him in time.

The sun was directly above her now. The heat was making her sweat and her clothes stick uncomfortably to her hot skin.

Everything ached as she pedalled furiously on. Her legs, her back. Her thoughts raced feverishly.

As the terrain became more rocky, cycling became impossible. Sophie laid down her bike and picked her way up and down the rocky ridges, calling out his name.

She walked on for another hour, clambering, slithering, stopping only to consult the sketched map, her throat sore from calling out his name.

And then, as she rounded a grassy mound, the huge mountain loomed directly ahead. Sophie stood, blinking up at it in awe.

Oh, Gareth, are you really up there somewhere? she murmured to herself. It was an impossible task. The mountain was vast, and there were ridges and craters and caves.

She slumped dejectedly to her knees. The best thing was to wait for the search party and then tell them that she thought this was where he was.

She fell back on to the warm grass, glad to rest a while, her eyes scanning the ridges, and then back across the valleys in the hope of sighting the search party. But the silence all around her grew heavy. She couldn't just sit and wait, she had to keep looking.

She got to her feet and stretched her aching limbs. Around the base of the mountain there seemed to be a fairly easy path. Perhaps she could circle the mountain and just keep looking and calling. At least she would be doing something, not just sitting.

She set off, picking her way around the lower slopes, calling out his name. Scrambling over boulders, grazing her hands and knees.

"Gareth! Gareth!"

Her neck ached from looking up and the sun blinded her each time her eyes squinted up at the vast grey rock.

"Gareth!"

And then, suddenly … "Sophie!"

"Gareth!" she shrieked, jumping for joy.

She could just see him, or rather she could see his leg, dangling over a ridge high up on the rock face.

"Gareth, I can see you," she yelled. "Are you all right?"

"My kneecap's dislocated," he called. His voice sounded tired, weak.

"What happened?"

"I fell."

"How long have you been stuck up there?"

"Since yesterday."

"Yesterday!" What a shame his gran didn't check her tea leaves yesterday instead of waiting till this morning, Sophie thought irritably.

"There's a search party on its way … Gareth … Gareth!"

She began to scramble up the rock face. If he lost consciousness he could easily roll over the edge. She needed to ease him further on to the ridge, until help came.

"Hold on, Gareth, I'm coming up. I've a bottle of water, I'll try and make you more comfortable."

"Feel funny, Sophie…" he managed to call down.

"Don't move. I'm coming."

"No … too dangerous."

"It'll be dangerous if you roll off that ledge. Just hang on." She stopped her clambering and studied the rock face for the best route to reach him. There were so many crevices and ridges, it didn't look too difficult a climb.

She continued on her way, finding foot holes without too much difficulty, and she made good progress.

She deliberately didn't look down, remembering her last attempt at climbing. There was no rope around her now should she fall.

Surprisingly, with so many ridges and crevices, it was even possible to sit for a moment to get her breath back every now and then. And she sat with her back against the warm rock, legs hanging over the ridge.

The view was quite breathtaking. The air

was so clean and fresh. And so perfectly silent except for the cry of the birds that had made their nests up here in the cracks.

"Are you still okay, Gareth?" she called up.

"A bit faint…"

"Don't move! I'll be with you in a few minutes."

She scrambled to her feet, carefully seeking out the next hand and foot holes by which to claw herself upwards.

"You're doing brilliantly, Sophie."

"You just concentrate on keeping alert," she shouted back.

She hauled herself up on to the next ridge. From here she could see Gareth. His knee lay twisted at a painful angle, his face grey, his lips tinged with blue.

As their eyes met across the sloping grey rock he grinned feebly. "My hero!"

Sophie laughed, despite the urge to tell him what a nuisance he was. Instead she flopped down on the wide ridge to catch her breath.

As she stretched out her arms, her hand blindly touched something straw-like and a hawk took flight from its nest with a great squawking cry. "Oh, help! I didn't see that!"

"You all right?"

"Yes, no panic. I just startled a hawk, that's all."

She inched further on to the ridge, avoiding the deep, narrow crevice running close by it.

"It's got a nest and eggs," Sophie called out. "It's all right, Mrs Hawk, I'm not going to harm your babies."

The bird circled overhead, its small round eyes fixed on the intruder and the precious nest.

Never having been so close to a hawk's nest, Sophie took a closer look at the eggs. They were nestled in a remarkable interweaving of twigs and ferns and … she frowned.

There was a sort of redness running through the nest, giving it a reddish colour overall. Fine red strands that the hawk had collected and woven into its nest.

Red hairs.

She slumped back against the rock, her eyes wide with alarm.

Around the opening of the crevice she saw more red hairs. Clinging to the rough stone, blowing in the wind.

Cautiously, with her heart drumming a fierce beat against her ribcage, Sophie reached into the black crack in the rock, fumbling, feeling with her outstretched fingers.

And then she felt something. Something quite different from cold damp rock.

It had a plasticky, leathery feel to it. Her fingers closed around it. Slowly she pulled.

At first there was some resistance. And then it came away and she brought it out into the sunlight.

It was a girl's trainer. About her size.

Discoloured and damp, but she could just make out the name written on the inside in blue ink.

Helena Bright!

CHAPTER 20

The search party, when it arrived, brought the two youngsters safely down from the rock face.

Gareth was suffering from exposure and a dislocated left kneecap, Sophie was suffering from shock.

Shortly afterwards, the mountain rescue brought down Helena Bright's body in their plastic zipped bag.

Sophie was back at Plas Dol-y-Mynydd house half an hour before everyone else had returned from canoeing.

A police sergeant had taken a statement from her. They left a policeman to tell David Meredith about the discovery.

Sophie lay on her bed, listening to the hubbub of her schoolfriends' chatter as they all made their way along to their rooms. Her door burst open and Ami, Jenny and Joanne descended on her with great whoops of delight.

Ami drew back first.

"Sophie, you've been crying."

"Canoeing wasn't that great," said Jenny, trying to console her pal. "You didn't miss much."

"Sophie, why was that policeman waiting?"

"The missing girl's been found."

"Where?" they all gasped.

Sophie explained briefly and Ami gave her a fierce hug. "Poor you. Oh! that must have been awful."

Despite all her good intentions, Sophie began to sob quietly again.

After dinner, David Meredith gathered everyone together in the day room. He looked grey and drawn. What he had to say had already been heard on the grapevine over dinner. No doubt he was aware of that, but felt duty bound to clear the air.

"I daresay most of you know anyway," he began, "but I think it's my duty to tell you officially. The youngster who vanished from here last year has been found." His voice quivered. "They brought her body down from the mountains this afternoon."

There was silence. Everyone looked at Sophie. She lowered her head.

The instructor continued. "Unfortunately for Sophie, she was the one to discover it, whilst trying to help a boy in difficulties."

His black eyes flashed their usual look of disapproval. "Although I'd given Sophie instructions not to wander away from here, she'd had a message informing her that a boy was in trouble. And while she should not have tried the climb herself after discovering him –" his face softened – "she did what she thought best under the circumstances."

Sophie blinked, amazed that he understood.

He looked her straight in the eye. "What you did, Sophie, took a great deal of courage."

Everyone in the room burst into a round of applause.

When that had died down, he continued. "For some time there has been speculation as to what happened to poor Helena Bright. Suspicions abounded that she might even have been murdered."

A murmur of voices went round the room.

"It would seem now," said David Meredith with a sigh, "that the poor girl went rock climbing alone, got into difficulties and took refuge in that crevice. Hypothermia must have set in and she slipped into a fatal coma."

His voice shook and he lowered his head. Mary Mooney instantly jumped up and wrapped her arms around him.

The Headmaster got to his feet. He cleared his throat. "Girls, this tragedy is something we can learn from. I hope you all see now why it's important that you follow the instructions given by the experts, and not go off doing your own thing."

"Yes, sir," everyone answered.

He put on a cheerful face. "Well then, let's try and put it all behind us and try to get back to normal. I know, let's get a game of some sort organized."

"How about murder in the dark?" Ami whispered, "No, perhaps not." She smiled sympathetically at Sophie as everyone dispersed. "Feeling any happier now, Soph? Now we know there never was any murder."

"Yes, I suppose so, and yet…"

"Oh, Sophie, stop! You've got to put all this behind you and start to enjoy yourself."

Sophie forced herself to smile. "You're right. Come on, let's go and help the Head organize a game."

Despite Sophie's deliberate attempts to forget everything, she couldn't budge a niggly feeling that something was wrong.

Logically, she told herself, it was because both Gareth and his gran had warned her that she was in danger by staying here. Surely that danger no longer existed.

There was only one way to find out.

She would visit Gareth's gran tomorrow. Get her palm read or her tea leaves or something.

Only then could she relax and know that the danger was truly over.

CHAPTER 21

There was no argument about her going to visit Gareth's gran the following morning. David Meredith organized it for everyone to spend the morning in the village to do some souvenir shopping.

After breakfast, they piled into the Land Rovers and drove via the winding lanes into the little village.

Sophie dragged Ami up the hill to the church and down the tiny leafy track by the churchyard.

Gareth's gran was delighted to see her. "Sophie! Come in, come in, child. I can't thank you enough for what you did for my Gareth yesterday."

"I did nothing, Mrs Jones," Sophie answered. "I was in such a state when I found that girl's shoe, all I could do was sit there and wait for help to arrive."

"You kept him going, child," she said, squeezing Sophie's hand. "You gave him hope to hang on, and not give in." She smiled knowingly, "Now you'll be wanting to see him?"

"Didn't the hospital keep him in?" Sophie asked, delighted.

"No, they patched him up and sent him home. Mind you, his leg's in plaster. Go on through. I'll make us a cuppa."

Ami was admiring the dozens of little potted herbs that littered the kitchen. "You go in, Soph, I'm not playing gooseberry."

Sophie went into Gareth's bedroom. He was propped up on three pillows and looked pale. His eyes hadn't lost their sparkle however. They still shone like pieces of silver.

"Hi! How are you feeling?"

He smiled weakly. "Leg hurts a bit, but otherwise I'm OK. How are you?"

146

She sat on the edge of his bed. "I can't get Helena out of my mind."

"Me neither," he said thoughtfully. "I can't understand why she'd go climbing on her own like that. She hated climbing."

"What?"

Gareth frowned. "Heights petrified her. She was so bad, they didn't even try to persuade her to go on the climbing expeditions. She used to stay behind and meet me."

Of course! The thing that had puzzled Sophie as she'd looked at the picture. Everyone else was all kitted out for rock climbing, while Helena was still in T-shirt and shorts, ready for a day of nothing more strenuous than sunbathing.

"It just doesn't make sense," Gareth added restlessly.

"No, it doesn't, does it," Sophie agreed.

"I suppose she died of exposure, stuck up there."

Sophie squeezed Gareth's hand. "Try not to dwell on it, Gareth. There's nothing we can do."

"At least I know now," he said sadly.

"You look tired, Gareth. Try and get some sleep."

"Will you come and see me again before you go home?"

"Of course. Now you just rest and get well."

As she reached the door, he said, "Take care, Sophie."

She wished he hadn't said it.

Back in the kitchen, his gran was pouring the tea. The old woman watched Sophie drinking it down, her sunken eyes eager for her to finish.

"You want to read the leaves, don't you?" said Sophie.

"And you want me to, don't you?"

Sophie nodded silently.

Ami peered into her own cup. "Great, will you read mine too? Tell me when I'll meet the man of my dreams!"

The old woman didn't reply but took Sophie's teacup, swirled it three times and upturned it on to the saucer.

Sophie watched, scarcely blinking, an uneasy feeling starting in the pit of her stomach.

When at last the old lady looked up, her eyes were deeply troubled. Sophie shivered.

"Nothing's changed for you, child. I still see danger awaiting you." She shook her head in exasperation. "If only I could see where the danger's coming from exactly."

She stared again, went to say something then shook her head. Finally she reached across and touched Sophie's long red hair. "I don't know, I think this has something to do with it."

"My hair?" Her voice died to a whisper. "Helena had red hair."

"Aye, I know that well enough, child."

There seemed nothing else to say and after thanking the old woman for the tea, and promising to return, Sophie and Ami wandered back down to the village.

"You're not going to take her seriously are you, Sophie?" scoffed Ami as they sat on a bench in the village square.

"I don't know."

"She's just a superstitious old woman."

"But she's been right so far."

Ami sighed. "A lucky guess. Oh, Soph, stop worrying. Helena Bright died by accident. There is no murderer."

"Then why am I in danger still?"

"Sophie, stop it!"

Paul Granger strode over from the news-agent's, eating an ice-cream. "Hi girls. Oh. Now what's up?"

Ami raised her eyebrows. "Ask her."

"Sophie?"

She took a deep breath. "We've been to see Gareth's gran. She read my tea leaves. It looks like I'm still in some sort of danger."

"Something to do with her hair."

He frowned.

Ami folded her arms, looking bored. "Is it possible there's a demon hairdresser around who doesn't like redheads?"

Neither Sophie nor Paul Granger laughed. Groaning, Ami got up and wandered across the road to get ice-creams.

"Do you think I'm being silly, Mr Granger?" Sophie asked. "Am I stupid paying any attention to an old woman's ravings?"

Mr Granger smiled kindly. "The village people seem to swear by her. She's never wrong by all accounts."

They fell silent as David Meredith strode across the village green towards them.

He looked troubled and Sophie wondered why he wasn't relieved that the Helena business had been solved. It ought to be a great weight off his mind. But if anything, he looked more serious than ever.

"Sophie, when we get back I'd like you to take me to the place where you found Helena," he said abruptly.

"Do I have to?" she asked uneasily. The thought of being alone with the instructor again renewed all her old fears.

"Mind if I come too?" Paul Granger asked casually and Sophie breathed a sigh of relief.

"Feel free," said the instructor. "We'll leave directly after lunch."

"Thank you," Sophie said to Paul Granger

once the instructor had gone.

"Better to be safe than sorry."

Sophie cast him an unhappy glance but said nothing.

Back at Dol-y-Mynydd house, everyone ate their sandwich lunches out on the lawns, enjoying the bright sunshine. The Headmaster was busy laying clues for a treasure hunt in the afternoon.

"Looking forward to the treasure hunt, girls?" Mary Mooney asked, joining Sophie and Ami on the grass. "Oh, has there been any further news on that poor girl?"

"What sort of news, miss?" Sophie asked.

"Well, cause of death, that sort of thing."

"Probably hypothermia," Ami suggested.

"But you don't know that for certain," Mary Mooney snapped. "I was asking Sophie if there was any definite news."

Both girls stared at her. It wasn't like Miss Mooney to loose her cool.

"No, there's been no news yet," Sophie told her quietly.

"You'll tell me, won't you, if you hear anything?"

"Yes, miss."

Miss Mooney smiled brightly. "Good. It'll be good when we know for sure. We can relax then."

"Yes, miss. But I'm sure it was nothing but a tragic accident," Sophie said, even though she wasn't sure if she even believed that herself.

"Yes, accidents happen all the time."

"Yes, miss," Sophie agreed, realizing suddenly that this whole business had affected everyone. For all she knew, Miss Mooney may have had her own suspicions about what happened to Helena Bright, although she obviously didn't suspect David Meredith.

The teacher's face lit up then as the instructor headed towards them. "Ah, David! I need a partner for this afternoon's treasure hunt. I'm sure we'd make an unconquerable pair."

But David Meredith's attention was focused upon Sophie. "Ready, Sophie? Sorry, Mary, you'll have to count me out of the treasure hunt. I'm tied up with something else."

Miss Mooney's face dropped. "That's all right," she murmured dejectedly. "I'm sure Mr Granger…"

"He's coming with us," Sophie interrupted, feeling terrible. Poor Miss Mooney.

"Him too?" Miss Mooney grated through clenched teeth.

"I'll be your partner, miss!" Ami offered enthusiastically.

"Thank you, Ami," Miss Mooney said stonily. "I'll see you in a few minutes then."

Sophie and Ami exchanged glances that clearly said, poor Miss Mooney!

By road, it was possible to get almost to the foot of the mountains and it was just a short walk to the actual rock face where Helena had been found.

Sophie, the instructor and Paul Granger all gazed up at the imposing mountain.

High above, Sophie spotted a hawk swoop down on the ridge and she pointed. "There, just where the hawk landed," she told them, glad that that bird hadn't deserted its nest because of all the commotion.

David Meredith looked at Sophie in amazement. "You climbed all the way up there?"

Sophie nodded.

"Good Lord!"

"It wasn't as difficult as it looked, really…"

"It must have taken an awful lot of nerve," suggested Paul Granger.

"I didn't think about it much," Sophie explained. "I was just worried in case Gareth lost consciousness and slipped off the ridge."

David Meredith studied her. "You don't like climbing, do you, Sophie?"

"No," she murmured, as her jumbled, troubled thoughts suddenly fell into place, sending a deathly chill through her body. "Do … do you mind if I go back to the Land Rover?"

"Of course not," said Paul Granger, "Meredith and I won't be long."

Sophie stumbled back to the waiting vehicle, her head spinning. Yet everything was suddenly becoming clear, horribly clear.

Helena hated climbing. Gareth had told her that. On the newspaper photograph, she had been dressed casually while everyone else was dressed for climbing. So why would she go climbing on her own? And without proper clothes or climbing boots? Why would she go climbing alone when she was supposed to be meeting Gareth? What possible reason could Helena have had for scrambling up there? Why climb when it frightened her so?

There was only one answer and she shivered violently.

Poor Helena never *climbed* the mountain at all.

She was killed beforehand. And someone hid her body up there thinking it would never be found. Or if it was found, it would look like an accident. As if she died of exposure.

A tragic accident.

And whoever killed Helena had to be someone experienced enough in mountaineering to hoist a dead body up the rock face.

Gareth? He was physically capable. But no, not Gareth.

And that left just one person.
David Meredith – their instructor!

CHAPTER 22

Dusk was creeping over the hills by the time they returned to the house. The sky was streaked red and black, the trees casting long black shadows across the grey earth.

Everyone else was already at dinner.

Ami dug her in the ribs. "Any more bodies?"

"Ha ha!" Sophie groaned. "How was the treasure hunt anyway?"

"Oh, that! A bundle of laughs, I don't think," complained Ami, popping half a fish finger into her mouth. "Mooning Mary was obviously still dreaming about our instructor because her mind was certainly not on the hunt. She was a right waste of time."

"Poor Miss Mooney." Sophie glanced about the dining room. "Where is she anyway?"

"Outside probably. I believe being lovesick can make you do strange thing – like losing your appetite. Do you think I could have her fish fingers?"

"Have mine," Sophie said, pushing her plate across the table. "I need to talk to her."

"What about?" Ami asked cheerfully, scraping the extra dinner on to her own plate.

"I'll tell you later," Sophie answered, and went in search of Miss Mooney.

The phone in the hall was ringing as Sophie walked along the corridor. She answered it. Someone wanted Paul Granger. Sophie returned to the dining room.

"You're wanted on the phone, Mr Granger."

He put down his knife and fork and followed her. She left him talking on the phone and went outside.

The moon wasn't up yet and great black clouds had drifted over the mountains, hanging like billowing sheets across the starless sky. The air was thick and clammy, as if a storm was brewing.

Sophie walked briskly, peering through the darkness for sight of Mary Mooney. She wasn't by the pond, or on the lawns. She called her name once or twice. There was no reply.

And then suddenly, a hand touched her shoulder and Sophie jumped.

"Oh! Miss Mooney, it's you," she gasped. "I was looking for you."

"Were you?" the teacher asked vaguely. There was a strange look in her eyes, as if her thoughts were far, far away.

"Are you all right, miss?"

Miss Mooney frowned, and then looked steadily into Sophie's face. "Yes, I'm all right." She pushed Sophie's hair back from her eyes. There was an impatient snap to her voice. "Why don't you fasten this back, Sophie, doesn't it get on your nerves?"

"No, miss, I'm used to it." She hesitated a moment. "Miss, could I talk to you?"

"Of course."

"It's about Helena." Sophie took a deep breath. She had to confide in someone. "Miss, I don't think Helena's death was an accident at all."

The teacher's frown deepened. "You don't?"

"No. You see, Helena hated climbing. She was terrified of heights, so there's no way she would have gone climbing alone. Especially without proper clothes and climbing boots."

"Go on," said Miss Mooney.

"I think someone killed her, and then hauled her body up the mountain and hid it."

Miss Mooney burst out laughing. "Oh, Sophie! I don't think so. Besides who would do such a thing, and why?"

Sophie looked steadily at her teacher. "Someone who didn't like her, someone who was angry with her maybe."

"Sophie, who are you implying?"

She swallowed hard. "It had to be an experienced climber, I ... I think it was Mr Meredith."

For a second Miss Mooney just stared at

her. And then she laughed again. "David! Oh, that's quite ridiculous."

Sophie chewed her lip anxiously. "I think it's even more ridiculous to believe that Helena would climb a mountain for no reason."

Miss Mooney put her arm around Sophie's shoulder and led her towards the Land Rover. "Sophie, have you spoken to anyone else about this?"

"Not yet, miss, but I think I should tell the police, don't you? Maybe they don't know how scared Helena was of heights. I must tell them, mustn't I?"

Mary Mooney slid into the driver's seat.

"Shall we go to the police now, miss? You could drive to the village."

Mary Mooney smiled and opened the passenger door for Sophie. "I think that's precisely what we should do. Even if just to clear David's name! Get in, Sophie."

Sophie hesitated. "Should I tell the Headmaster? He might wonder where we are."

"No, Sophie, if David is guilty, not that I

162

believe that for one moment, we don't want to alert his suspicions, do we? Come along, I'll take full responsibility for your absence."

Sophie felt as if a great weight had been lifted from her shoulders. Eagerly, she climbed into the Land Rover beside her teacher.

As the headlights cut through the darkness, Sophie glanced sideways at her teacher. Miss Mooney was taking the news of David being a possible murderer very well, considering how she liked him.

It was almost dark now, and the mountain range loomed closer as they drove along the bumpy lane.

Sophie frowned. "Miss, this isn't the way to the village."

"I know another route," Miss Mooney explained, adding, "firstly, though, I think you should show me where you found that unfortunate girl. If we can come up with some other answer rather than accuse David of murder, I shall be greatly relieved."

"You don't think it was him, do you, miss?"

Mary Mooney gave Sophie a strange cold glance. "I *know* it wasn't him."

Sophie looked away, staring through the window at the black rock pitted with caves and crevices that loomed straight ahead. No wonder Miss Mooney was taking this so well, she wouldn't for one moment think her darling David could be a murderer. She was simply humouring her.

Sophie began to wish that she'd gone straight to the police without telling anyone of her thoughts. Mary Mooney stopped the Land Rover and got out, beckoning Sophie to join her. Sophie shivered. A cool wind had sprung up now, chilling her, whistling through the rocks, rustling the coarse grass. And shadows crept out of the earth, stretching long and black like cloaks, wrapping themselves around her. A suffocating blackness seemed to engulf her.

"I don't know if I can show you exactly where I found Helena in the dark, miss. Could we go on to the village instead? I could show you the place tomorrow."

But Miss Mooney was striding on ahead, clambering over the rocks as sure-footed as a mountain goat.

Sophie tried to catch her up, hating the eerie silence of the mountains, hating the shadows. But she stumbled on the rocks, and had to feel her way carefully.

"Miss, wait for me… Miss! Miss Mooney, where are you?"

Sophie stopped, struggling to balance on a large smooth rock as she squinted through the blackness for a sight of her teacher.

"Miss Mooney, I can't see you!"

Sophie was about to take another step, when Miss Mooney's voice echoed through the gloom.

"Sophie!"

Still Sophie couldn't see her. "Where are you?"

"Up here, Sophie."

Sophie stopped and peered upwards. To her amazement, she could just make out the shadowy form of someone standing on a rough rocky ledge just above her head.

"Miss! How did you get up there?"

"It wasn't difficult. Come on up, Sophie, I want you to show me where you found Helena."

Sophie looked about her. It was the spot. The exact place she had begun her climb up to Gareth and poor Helena. But how could Miss Mooney have known that?

An icy chill crawled up Sophie's spine. Miss Mooney had driven straight here, whereas she'd had to direct David Meredith earlier...

And Miss Mooney had been to Dol-y-Mynydd before, that's how she knew the instructor...

Helena's school was on the north-east coast ... Miss Mooney had a north-eastern accent...

She began to back away, terror crawling through her. All this time, she had thought the instructor was the murderer...

"Don't you run away from me, Sophie!" Mary Mooney's voice suddenly rang out, harsh and bitter.

"It was you!" Sophie cried out in alarm,

staggering backwards. "You! But why?"

Miss Mooney was towering over her from the rough ledge; her eyes were wild, insane. Her voice was thick with venom and spite, her high pitched shrieks echoing across the valleys as she screamed down at Sophie.

"Why? You ask me why?" she raged. "I'll tell you why. It's always the same. First my fiancé. He fell for another woman and left me. And then David. Always too preoccupied with the troublesome ones to notice me!"

"He's … he's a busy man…" Sophie stammered, trying to feel her way backwards.

"It was exactly the same last time!"

"What do you mean?"

A cold smile spread across the teacher's face. It contorted her features and made her look hideous.

Sophie stumbled and fell.

"Yes, last time. Last year. I used to teach up north, St. Mark's Convent."

"Helena Bright's school!" gasped Sophie, slithering on the smooth rocks as she tried to get to her feet.

"Yes, Helena Bright. Mischievous Helena Bright. Always the centre of attention. Keeping David occupied. I wanted David Meredith then, but just like now, and like with my fiancé, there was always some other younger, prettier girl getting all the attention…"

Sophie's blood ran deathly cold as she saw suddenly that Mary Mooney had raised a massive rock above her head, and was about to send it crashing down on to her.

Mary Mooney's voice rose. "And they've all had long red hair!"

With one final shriek of fury, Mary Mooney sent the massive rock hurtling down at Sophie.

CHAPTER 23

Throwing herself sideways at the last second, Sophie just avoided the rock. It crashed inches from her head, sending sparks and a shower of granite splinters into the air.

Miss Mooney's shriek of anger became one of frustration as she started to scramble down the rock face. But Sophie was on her feet and running.

Heart pounding, Sophie slithered and stumbled on the uneven rocks, trying to get away from her crazed teacher. But the blackness hampered her escape. Rocks tripped her time and again, sending her sprawling on the ground, forcing her to claw her way on hands and knees more often than on her feet. And Miss Mooney was coming after her. Sophie could hear the crunch of stones beneath the teacher's feet. Glancing back, she saw her shadowed outline, and realized with terror that the teacher was more agile over rocks than she was.

Sophie ran on, dragging herself to her feet each time she stumbled. Her breathing was ragged and painful. Fear had dried her throat and her heart seemed to be trying to beat its way out of her ribcage.

Through frightened eyes, Sophie glimpsed something far off in the darkness. Two spots of light.

With lungs fit to burst, Sophie raced on towards the lights. Behind her, Miss Mooney's quickening footsteps were becoming louder as she closed the distance between them.

The lights seemed to be growing larger, brighter, as if they were moving towards her. And then Sophie heard the growl of an engine and realized through her terror that the lights were car headlights. But Miss

Mooney was oblivious, and her shrieking filled the night air, almost drowning out the roar of the engine.

On and on Sophie ran, forcing her legs to move swifter, sensing the insane woman getting closer and closer. Glancing back, Sophie saw her teacher's face, crazed out of all recognition, wild eyes, her mouth screaming out her fury.

The car was still hurtling towards them when Sophie felt a fierce force push her from behind. Her legs buckled and she fell headlong into the dust. Miss Mooney fell on top of her.

Sophie managed to turn and saw in the blaze of headlights the jagged rock in the teacher's hand as she raised her arm in fury. And then a screech of brakes, a blurring of figures lunging at the insane woman. Two figures, David Meredith and Paul Granger. Together they managed to drag the screaming and kicking Miss Mooney away from Sophie.

The struggle ended swiftly, and to Sophie's amazement – and the instructor's, judging by

the look on his face – Paul Granger produced
a set of handcuffs and expertly applied them
to Miss Mooney's wrists.

CHAPTER 24

Much later that evening the commotion had died down. After they had delivered Mary Mooney to the local police station and she was safely locked up, everyone returned to Dol-y-Mynydd house. The girls were all in bed, and the Headmaster was waiting anxiously at the door.

Sophie gripped the mug of hot tea that he had poured. Her hands were trembling only a little now. The instructor looked across the table to Paul Granger and grinned. "You know, I was positive I'd seen you before. You were one of the police officers originally on Helena's case, weren't you?"

"Minus the beard," explained Paul Granger, alias Detective Inspector Granger, from the north-east branch of the police force. "One of our boys has accompanied every school trip since Helena's disappearance."

"Well, blow me down!" murmured the Headmaster, shaking his head. "You had me fooled. I'd say you could get a permanent job as a teacher if you ever decided to leave the force!"

"Thank you, sir," Paul Granger smiled. "I'm sorry I couldn't tell you what was going on. But I had to make my cover foolproof. I couldn't risk being discovered." He glanced again at the instructor. "It's not that we didn't trust *you*, David, but the prime suspect did boil down to someone local. We were just doing our job. I thought I'd blown it that first night when you gave me a funny look."

Sophie thought back to all the funny looks David Meredith had given her.

"Yes, I thought I knew you," remarked David Meredith. "And as for you, Sophie, when I first saw you, I thought you were Helena. Then, when you said someone was outside your window that first night I just had an awful feeling that history would repeat itself. That's why I've been keeping a close eye on you."

"And I thought you were sizing me up as your next victim," Sophie said awkwardly.

"I had the feeling that's what was bothering you," David Meredith said. "You probably thought it was me outside your window that first night."

"I wondered for a while. But I realize it must have been Gareth. He thought I was Helena too, you see. By the way, which of you had been out in the grounds that night and left wet footprints on my floor?"

"That was me," Paul Granger admitted. "Just checking things over. I heard your shrieks half a mile away."

Sophie nodded. "But when the real danger came, I didn't make a peep. If you two hadn't arrived when you did, she would have killed me too. Thank goodness you came when you did. But what made you follow us? And how did you know where we were?"

David Meredith set down his cup. "Well, Sophie, when you showed me where you found Helena, I realized she wouldn't have dared to climb all that way up. And that left one alternative…"

Sophie nodded. "You came to the same conclusion as me, that someone killed her and hid her body up there."

He looked desperately sad. "That's right, and it had to be someone skilled enough to do just that. I knew it wasn't me, and I was aware that Mary Mooney was a good enough mountaineer to do it. I just couldn't believe she would do such a thing."

"I know," murmured Sophie. "I trusted her too."

Paul Granger interrupted. "Remember that phone call for me this evening, Sophie?"

"Yes."

"It was the Police. Forensic had come up with the same conclusion as David here. When I told him what they'd discovered, he took off like the wind."

The instructor looked grave.

"As soon as Paul told me about the phone call, I realized there really was a murderer at large. The fact that you, Miss Mooney and a Land Rover had disappeared made me act quickly. The murderer often returns to the scene of the crime, so we drove to the mountain first."

"Thank goodness you did," Sophie murmured, lowering her eyes. "Although after all the trouble I've caused you, I'm surprised you came after me at all."

"Sophie!" David Meredith sighed, grinning. "Since you arrived here, chasing you, keeping my eye on you, watching what you're up to, has become an unbreakable habit with me!"

On impulse, Sophie wrapped her arms around his neck and hugged him. "Thank goodness it wasn't a habit you decided to break. At least not tonight!"

He ruffled her hair. "From now on I think it's a habit I can relax a little. After all, you've got another week here. Let's see if you can enjoy it."

Sophie grinned. "I will – so long as I never, ever have to go mountain climbing again!"

Hippo Fantasy

Lose yourself in a whole new world, a world where anything is possible – from wizards and dragons, to time travel and new civilizations . . . Gripping, thrilling, scary and funny by turns, these Hippo Fantasy titles will hold you captivated to the very last page.

The Night of Wishes
Michael Ende (author of *The Neverending Story*)

Malcolm and the Cloud-Stealer
Douglas Hill

The Wednesday Wizard
Sherryl Jordan

Ratspell
Paddy Mounter

Rowan of Rin
Emily Rodda

The Practical Princess
Jay Williams

Our favourite Babysitters are detectives too! Don't miss the new series of Babysitters Club Mysteries:

Available now:

No 1: Stacey and the Missing Ring
When Stacey's accused of stealing a valuable ring from a new family she's been sitting for, she's devastated – Stacey is *not* a thief!

No 2: Beware, Dawn!
Just *who* is the mysterious "Mr X" who's been sending threatening notes to Dawn and phoning her while she's babysitting, *alone?*

No 3: Mallory and the Ghost Cat
Mallory thinks she's solved the mystery of the spooky cat cries coming from the Craine's attic. But Mallory can *still* hear crying. Will Mallory find the *real* ghost of a cat this time?

No 4: Kristy and the Missing Child
When little Jake Kuhn goes missing, Kristy can't stop thinking about it. Kristy makes up her mind. She *must* find Jake Kuhn . . . wherever he is!

No 5: Mary Anne and the Secret in the Attic
Mary Anne is curious about her mother, who died when she was just a baby. Whilst rooting around in her creepy old attic Mary Anne comes across a secret she never knew . . .

No 6: The Mystery at Claudia's House
Just what is going on? Who has been ransacking Claudia's room and borrowing her make-up and clothes? Something strange is happening at Claudia's house and the Babysitters are determined to solve the mystery . . .

No 7: Dawn and the Disappearing Dogs
Dawn decides to try her hand at *pet*sitting for a change, and feels terrible when one of her charges just . . . disappears. But when other dogs in the neighbourhood go missing, the Babysitters know that someone is up to no good . . .

No 8: Jessi and the Jewel Thieves
Jessi is thrilled to be taking a trip to see Quint in New York, and thinks that nothing could be more exciting. But when they overhear a conversation between jewel thieves, she knows that the adventure has only just begun . . .

No 9: Kristy and the Haunted Mansion
Travelling home from a game, Kristy and her all-star baseball team are stranded when a huge storm blows up. The bridges collapse, and the only place they can stay looks – haunted . . .

No 10: Stacey and the Mystery Money
When Stacey gets caught with a fake banknote, the Babysitters are astounded. Can *counterfeiters* really have come to Stoneybrook? The Babysitters have to solve the mystery, clear Stacey's name *and* save their reputation . . .

Look out for: